"With *Kings of the Dead*, Tony Faville blurs the line between our real world and an apocalyptic nightmare world of zombies. And makes that fun. *Kings of the Dead* is wild and weird, dangerous and delightful!"

—Jonathan Maberry, NY Times bestselling
author of *Rot & Ruin* and *Patient Zero*

"For every zombiphile who's ever imagined how it might go down if the living dead came shambling into their world... they're here!"

—David Dunwoody, author of *Empire* and *Empire's End*

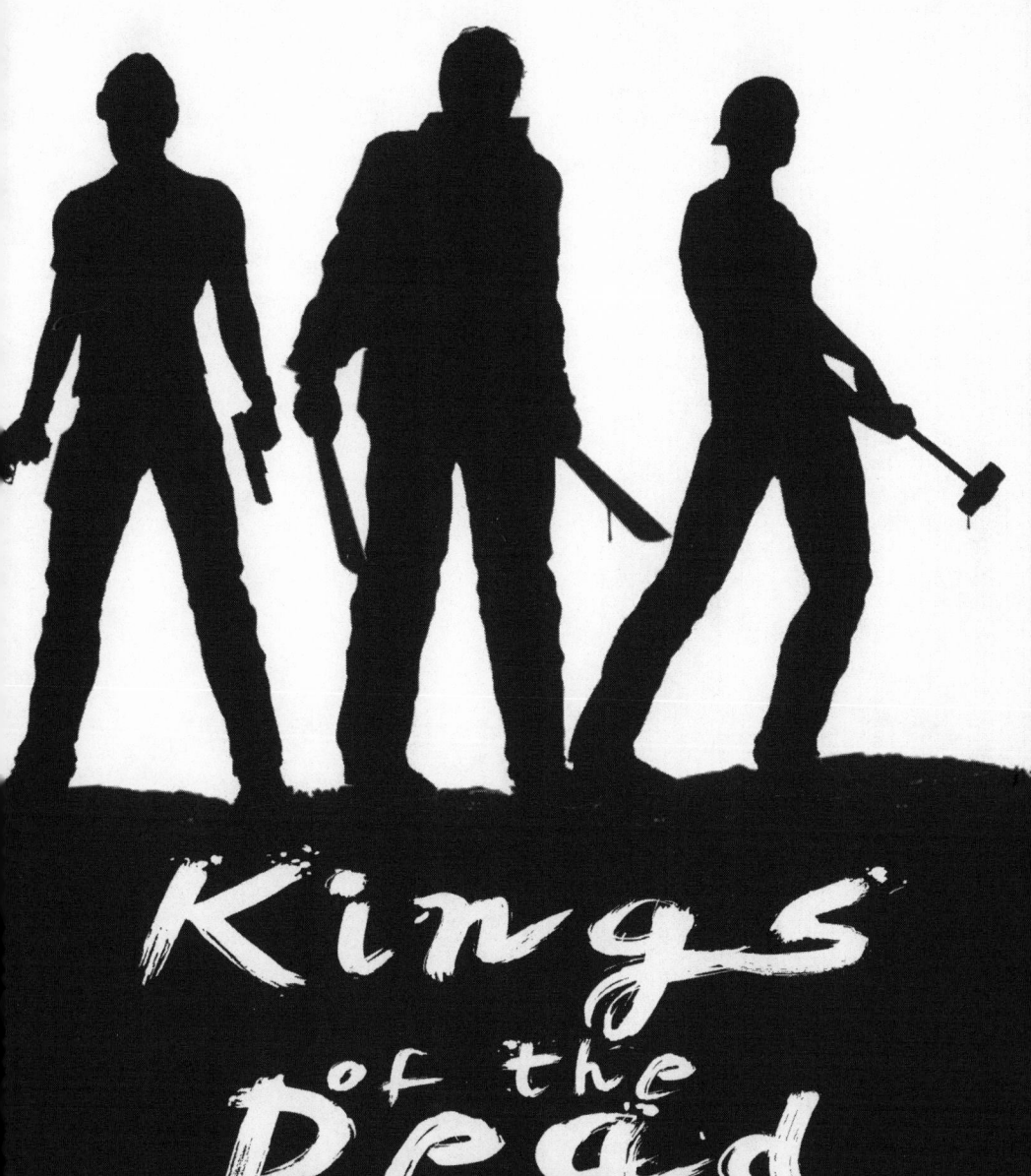

Kings
of the
Dead

TONY FAVILLE

A PERMUTED PRESS book
published by arrangement with the author
ISBN-13: 978-1-934861-83-7
ISBN-10: 1-934861-83-9

Dedicated to my wife, Heather.
If she had not said "Yes you can," I wouldn't have.

Darren —

I appreciate your hospitality.

Thanks,

MAY 15, 2009

My name is Cole Helman, and while I have gone by many nicknames in the past, Doc Hardball and Chef just to name a few, these days my friends have given me a new nickname.

I am Zombie Hunter Cole.

Looking back on things, I never thought it would happen to me...

It's funny, I always thought I would be writing that in one of those tacky Penthouse Forum letters. You know the stories, they always start out "I went to check the mail and next thing I know, I was in bed getting it on with the mail lady, the MILF next door and a couple of cheerleaders." Now, I am not saying that anything like that situation ever happened to me, but I can almost guarantee you, it never happened to the other people that wrote those letters either.

No, what I never thought would happen, wound up being exactly what happened about ten weeks ago.

The dead started to walk.

It actually started almost a year ago with the swine flu pandemic. The damn virus just kept mutating to the point that "it" started to kill with rampant wholesale, and then those it killed started to get up and kill. Before we knew it, it was like one of those shampoo commercials, I'll tell four people, and they'll tell four people and on and on. Only in this reality you change the "tell" to kill.

It took months for things to get to that stage though and to be honest with you, I can tell you exactly when it started happening. It was when they started giving the vaccinations.

It was the shots! The damn shots triggered the final stage of the viral mutation, the one that caused people to die, only to reanimate shortly after death.

Look, all I am saying is that I have not met anyone since it all started that actually received the shot.

Every single person I knew that got the vaccine is dead. Every one of those people got back up after dying and some of them I had to put down.

Maybe I need to back up a little bit here to let you know a little about my history. In the early 1980's I saw a movie late one night that changed my life, *Dawn of the Dead* by the zombie master himself, George A. Romero. Since that evening I have watched every single zombie movie I could get my hands on, I read every book, comic book, or journal, and listened to every podcast, etc.

It was never a situation of hoping it was real, or even dreaming about a zombie rising. No, it was nothing more than the fact that I just really dug the entire concept of the Zombie genre. It was the "what if" scenario that really got to me.

What if the dead rose?

What if zombies were real?

What if the world went to shit?

I started "preparing" for this to happen several years ago. At first it was just stockpiling some food, water, weapons, first aid, miscellaneous supplies, and eventually, if not most importantly, people.

I was never looking to build an army around me, I simply wanted to spend my time with people that were of like minds. People with skill sets that would be necessary in a PAW, or post-apocalyptic world. Construction, medicine, farming, shooting, tactical operators, mechanics, people like that.

Now don't get me wrong, it's like I mentioned above, We NEVER thought zombies were really going to get back up and start doing the hokey-pokey. That was just the stuff we used to make what we were doing more interesting. I look back at when I first started working with my wife to get her prepared for a concealed weapons permit. She had a difficult time dealing with the idea of training to shoot someone. It was only after I turned the training into more of a zombie preparation concept that she really started to get into the training.

At first, we were making these preparations based on the potential of natural and social disasters. Earthquakes, fires, floods, anarchy, whatever you can envision.

I would not consider any of us to be "survivalists", at least not in the media's stereotypical definition of the word. We are good people, family people, relatively normal people that are, or were willing to do whatever it takes to survive. Our biggest failure, if you will, is that our earthquake never came.

Zombies sure as hell did though.

Before it all started we had our designated bug out location, or BOL. It is a nice, quiet, wooded area with fresh running water and far away from the big cities. That location is exactly where we have been for the past 8 weeks.

Before things got totally crazy in the city we held a meeting and made the decision that it was time to go. Within days we had loaded up our stuff and got the hell out of town.

Now, didn't I say the dead started to rise ten weeks ago? And did I not just say we headed out 8 weeks ago?

Yeah, I did. We did not wait around to see how the government would handle the situation. We had made our preparations and wanted to get out of there before those who had nothing to prepare, decided to help themselves to what we had collected.

The time for preparation is not when a ghoul is gnawing on your throat or pulling your entrails from a hand-torn gash in your abdomen. No, the time for preparation is before that happens.

We could see the signs. We *knew* what was coming. If we were wrong, and the government had been able to hold the line against the walking dead, then we would all be taking a nice long camping trip and looking for jobs when we came back out of the woods.

The thing is though, we were not wrong. Things got worse, daily.

People used to laugh at us because we were a bunch of zombie geeks, fan boys, survival nuts, gun freaks. You name it, at some point in time, some clown that thought he was better than us had labeled us as such.

These days we have a new label, one that we wear with pride-we are the Kings of the Dead and we will survive.

MAY 16, 2009

Let me take a moment to talk about these undead zombie-like creatures. Hey, you know what? I am here, I am living it, and I think I will call them whatever in the hell I want to call them.

Zombies.

There, I did it, I called them zombies.

Now then, what did the movies teach us about zombies?

I quote, *"they are the walking dead brought back to life by radioactive space dust, the fact that hell ran out of vacancies, space aliens, voodoo priests and various other sundry choices. They eat the flesh of the living, whether it is brains, arms, necks, intestines, you name it. They either shamble or haul ass depending on who is telling the story."*

In almost every zombie movie I ever watched, you must destroy the brain or do enough damage to their body in order to ultimately destroy them. If we take the zombies from the *Return of the Living Dead* series of movies, they speak, they move quickly, use radios, costumes and tools, and destroy every damn thing in their path. In all stories, a bite from one of the infected will take out one of the living. I have even seen some stories where a simple scratch from one would be enough to infect a person.

Now I can hear you now, "A scratch?!" Yes, a scratch. Think about it for a moment, what happens to the skin when you get a bad enough scratch... that's right, you bleed. Now, what if the individual

4

that is scratching you is a dead, decaying, reeking bone bag? When he scratches you, there is a very good chance that one or two of his own fingernails will be pulled off during the scratch.

Did you ever rip off a fingernail? What happened, other than it hurt like hell? That's right again... it bled.

What happens when you combine two liquids? They mix, and in this case, infected blood mixes with non-infected blood. Does the infected blood become non-infected blood? No, it sure as hell does not. The non-infected blood becomes infected.

Are you beginning to understand how a scratch could infect you? Good, let's move along.

So, what do I know about these zombies?

Our zombies were caused by the H1N1 Vaccine... that has to be what did it. Okay, sure, I'm not a scientist and I don't know that for sure, but it is all I have to go on, and I am holding on tight to the idea.

Some of the guys have even joked around a bit and called it the H1Z1 virus. Obviously, the Z is for zombie.

That's cool, whatever it takes to keep them going.

Oh, my zombies? Yeah, they don't run.

Let me just say a couple of things about this fact.

Number one, THANK GOD!!

Number two, this is actually to be expected. When a person dies, the body starts to break down immediately, and things like tendons lose their elasticity and muscles stop working. Since these creatures are obviously dying before they turn, the natural order of things has not changed and will not change.

I don't care what the bug is in their head that is making them get up and move, they are still dead. They are not going to run or be able to do anything more complex than a simple grab at a potential food source.

I have seen handfuls of them attempting to run since this all started and every time I have seen the same results. It's typically the achilles tendon that fails first, then the knees and then the hamstring.

You may have the mother of all viruses in your brain making you do all sorts of crazy shit, but without a complete set of working wheels beneath you, you're not walking anywhere, let alone running with all the tenacity of a decathlete.

Back to my zombies—they eat flesh. They seem to resort to the most primal instincts of survival and go for the most vulnerable spots to feed by doing everything in their power to get a bite into any part of you they can.

One of the things I learned in the multitude of self defense courses I have taken over the years, is that you have to be prepared for every fight to wind up on the ground. Even when dealing with humans you take a chance on getting bit or scratched. Do you really want to get into a ground fight with a creature that only bites or scratches?

Trust me on this, the best defense is a good offense. If the opportunity to shoot one of these things from a distance is presented to you, take it! Never let a zombie get within striking distance of you. If a zombie gets closer than ten feet to me, then I have screwed up and let him get too close to me. If you let one get that close to you, don't do like you have seen them do in the movies and start punching them.

Please, for God's sake, don't start punching them. Were you ever in a fight and punched someone in the mouth? If you had, the chances are you would completely understand why I am telling you to not punch them in the face. Zombies have teeth in their mouth, that is what makes them so dangerous. You punch them in the mouth, you risk their teeth penetrating through their own lips and into your knuckles. Trust me, I have seen this happen in bar fights between two drunk and stupid but otherwise healthy human beings.

If you have to resort to close combat with a zombie, take out their legs. Seriously, sweep the leg Daniel-san. They can already barely stand up of their own volition, what do you think they will do if you kick them in the side of the knee with your size 11 combat boots? They will fall down, and once they are down, take that size 11 boot one more time and stomp their head until you hit pavement.

One of the last things I want to do is to have to put someone down because they thought punching a zombie in the face was a good idea. Don't get me wrong, it may be one of the last things I want to do, but I sure as hell will do it.

Taking them down? Well, as we all know a head-shot works quite effectively. I have seen a few go down where I was truly unable to discern if it was due to a successful head-shot. With that being said, I'm not going to waste any ammo with body shots on the off chance it will work this time.

We have one guy with the Kings by the name of Gabe. Gabe is a bit of a renaissance man much like myself. Former military, and since the Navy he has bounced (sometimes quite literally... he was a bouncer for years) around doing this, that and the other job. The guy is wicked with this Nordic axe he keeps strapped around his chest and hanging from his back. I have seen him cleave a zombie practically from the top of its head to its waist. Honestly, without the proper sanitation or at least a good shave and a haircut, Gabe is looking more and more like a Viking every day. I guess it was all those years in the SCA that got him into that frame of mind.

Anyway, that is what I know about our zombies to date. They shamble, they eat the flesh of the living, and they die.

If you get bit or scratched, *vaya con dios amigo*, we will miss you when you are gone.

In a world where the dead walk the earth, you have to have separation of emotions. There will be time for mourning, someday. For now though, you do what you have to do. The creature walking toward you with its flesh falling from its bones, blood, vomit and other bodily fluids covering it from head to toe is no longer Uncle Ed or Grandma Edna. They are a pox on humanity and they must be eliminated. End of story.

Before I close out this entry, I want to explain myself to whoever is reading this. And yeah, for the record, I am hoping that it is a book publisher reading this because we won back our world and my journal is getting ready to go on the New York Times Best Seller List.

Yeah, right, like that will ever happen.

Most likely, you are some poor schlub who was lucky enough to have outlasted me, and you have found my gear and decided to read it before you either ate it or burned it.

If that is the case, then that is why I am writing this. I want you to learn from my successes and my failures. Inevitably, we all make mistakes. If you are able to glean even one gem of knowledge out of this that helps you survive one more day, then hot damn, I have succeeded.

So please, bear with me as I use this tool to maintain my sanity. Learn about me, my friends, our mutual enemy and how to survive. Who knows? Maybe someday someone will use it to look back and figure out a way to keep it from ever happening again.

MAY 17, 2009

Zombie extermination... that's what we call killing, and to steal a line from many movies, killing is our business and business is good.

Okay, just to be fair, in the past 8 weeks we have not seen more than a couple thousand zombies. Like I said, we got out of the big cities early. The fact remains, however, that we have seen that many in our travels into smaller towns and frankly, that worries me. If we are 60 miles out of downtown and still seeing that many, then what the hell do the cities look like?

Last I can recall there was something like 2,000,000 plus people living in the Portland metropolitan area.

Do the math, and that is a lot of damn zombies.

Because of that we have fortified our encampment with walls, trenches, fighting positions and kill zones. Hell, we have so many outward facing spikes that if anyone were still flying around up there, we would look like some kind of sea urchin from the air.

One of the nice things about the kill zones we have created is that they are narrow enough to prevent any kind of surge attack and afford us the opportunity to take our time and get that important head shot on one zombie at a time. With four such kill zones around the camp, technically, we would only need four defenders in the event of a mass attack.

So far the most we have seen at the camp at any one time numbered less than a dozen. With that few in numbers, I would have to assume they were people trying to get out of town themselves, only they left a little too late.

Our weapons are what you would typically expect to see: a handful of AR-15's, a few AK-47's, shotguns, SKS rifles, a lot of Ruger 10-22's and of course a bunch of high capacity handguns; 9mm, .45 acp being predominant. There are a few specialty guns as well, like my Smith and Wesson Model 66 .357 magnum double action revolver. I always liked this gun as it was the exact same revolver my uncle had when he was a police officer, and now this one never leaves my hip.

There is no room for discussion of caliber these days. Nobody is touting one over the other, much like the AR *vs*. AK debate. The debate is done. Either round, the 5.56 (AR) or the 7.62x39 (AK) will both punch through a rotted zombie skull as easily as through a watermelon. Yes, the AK round will punch through a helmet and the skull, but they are both effective weapons for killing the undead.

Allow me to go back to what I was talking about earlier in regards to what happens to a human body when it dies, with emphasis on the fact that its flesh starts to decay. Obviously, the same thing starts to happen to its bones. They begin to decalcify, the marrow dries and the bones become lighter and weaker, and not as resilient as they once were. This goes for the skull as well.

What that means for us is that the venerable .22 long rifle round, in a solid form, has become one hell of a potent close range zombie killer. That hot little round only needs to penetrate into the cranial cavity and then it's free to ricochet around in there, scrambling the gray matter.

Remember when Reagan was shot by Hinckley? He was shot with a .22 long rifle round fired from a pistol. The round found a way through the rib cage and then bounced around inside his chest, fortunately missing the heart.

The same thing happens with a zombie. I have to admit, it is interesting to watch a zombie take a head shot and see his reaction before enough damage is done and it hits the ground. Sure, we have greater potential need for a follow-up shot, but since we have ten times as many rounds of .22 as we do anything else, it really is a moot point.

For now, most of us are sticking to the .22 for our every day zombie killing and saving our bigger caliber stuff for a real shit hitting the fan situation or for the pending human factor.

I'll talk about the human factor in my next entry, time permitting.

Other than firearms, blades have been working quite well, tomahawks, small shovels and machetes for the most part. Like they say, the nice thing about a blade is they never need reloading. What they do need though is more physical strength than most people realize, and they do jam. Obviously they don't jam in the same sense of the word as a firearm, but unless you get a clean cut all the way through, you will have a jam on your hands.

I saw a kid go down a couple of weeks past because his QVC Shopping Channel katana got stuck in a zombie's skull. He tried getting it out of the skull as other zombies were closing in on him but he couldn't. He had used all of his strength just getting the killing blow, let alone having anything left for any other zombies in the immediate area. Unfortunately, he was already bitten before we were able to take out the zombies surrounding him.

Situation with a long sword is this, even a master swordsman who spends his entire life practicing his art will grow tired long before he runs out of necks to sever. How well do you think someone who bought their sword off of eBay in the event of the apocalypse will do? One, two, three strikes... and you are out!

I have one blade that I use as a back-up weapon; a World War II U.S. Navy Hospital Corpsman Bolo. Big, thick, heavy and if I didn't know better, I would swear it was made for killing zombies. One of my old Master Chiefs told me a tale of a Japanese soldier being taken out by one of these knives, cleaved from the left side of the neck all the way through the body to the right hip. I used to think it was nothing more than an old sea story, until the day I did it to a zombie. It was like a hot knife slicing through butter.

Oh yeah, that old hunk of steel is on my left hip at all times these days.

Truthfully, there is no big science to killing zombies. Aim for the head, do massive damage, and take them down. Forget military tactics, these are like no guerilla or insurgent forces anyone has ever faced. They are not fighting for land or religion, nor do they feel pain or suffer from hot or cold. They exist simply to eat and to propagate their virus, adding to their numbers. You simply need to kill them before they kill you.

That is where the government made their mistakes. In case you did not hear how things went down, our military tried fighting them like they fight anyone else and they got their asses handed to them in cities all across the nation.

Look, an M1 Abrams tank may be one hell of a killing machine, but as mentioned previously, the human factor took hold. Friendly fire took out almost as many of the military as the zombies did. There is nothing worse in the middle of a firefight than to all of a sudden no longer be able to tell the difference between friend and foe. A soldier panics—and who wouldn't panic seeing their squad mates being eaten—and fires wildly into a crowd of what he believes to be zombies. It happens. No matter how well trained or prepared you are, shit happens.

I remember just a few weeks back when we caught some radio traffic from the closest military checkpoint. Sounds of intense battle were interspersed with commands, screams, and cries for help. We sat there and listened to it for about 15 minutes before I reached over and turned the knob to static. There is nothing we could have done to help. Even if we had been able to make it out of here and to their location, it would have been too little, too late.

MAY 20, 2009

A member of the group left yesterday, and I have to admit I could have picked a much better person to lose than Lenny. He was an old Navy guy much like me, and even spent time after the Navy in the Coast Guard performing rescue work in New Orleans after hurricane Katrina.

After he got out of the military, he entered law enforcement and was a damn good deputy. He has the classic look of a police officer, standing six foot four, around 260 pounds and with a heart of gold. Not to mention he was a damn fine shooter with a ton of great experience, and was a real cool operator.

I can understand his leaving a little bit, he had been kind of disconnected since this entire thing started. Losing your wife and kids will do that to you.

The story he told us was that he and his wife had argued about getting the vaccines. She wanted them for the kids and he obviously did not want them. Two days later she came home from the clinic with all of the kids vaccinated. Four days later and they were all dead.

Twenty minutes later, Lenny walked out of his house and headed to the woods.

He was the first one at the bug out location and had most of the work done in the first days. In retrospect, we would not be in the condition we are in now if not for him and the work he did.

A few nights back he came to me and said he had picked up survivors on the radio that needed help, and he was thinking about going to retrieve them. We talked about it for a while and agreed that it would be something we need to discuss as a group. We know all too well that we have to be careful and only let the right people in to the group.

It wound up that I was the last one to see him in the camp, I was relieving him of his watch and he headed off towards his shelter. Nobody has seen him since.

I talked to Harley about it this morning over breakfast, and he told me that Lenny never touched the radio. Harley is very sensitive about who uses his radio and said that he has not picked up anyone in weeks.

What the hell, Lenny?

MAY 22, 2009

I want to talk about the Human Factor. You have likely read those two words a couple of times already and are curious about what I mean by it.

Looking back on so many of the zombie movies we used to watch, the best stories always had more to do with the survivors than it did the actual zombies.

Fuck the zombies man; they are nothing more than set pieces in this drama. Their purpose is to eat the flesh of the living, that's it. It's the people that make a good story. Their successes, their failures, their histories, their interactions with others, hell, even their dialogue. That's the stuff I'm talking about!

Keep in mind though, the human factor takes many different forms. I find it to be either the good or the bad in people. It's what drives someone to do something they would never have done in any other situation. Again, whether we are talking doing something extraordinarily good, or something maliciously heinous, it can be counted as the human factor.

Take my definition of a hero; they are just an ordinary person that has been placed into an extraordinary situation and finds they have risen to the occasion.

As I said above, it can also be the bad in people. Take a person with a broken moral compass for example. They steal, they abuse loved ones, or simply put, they display severe anti-social behavior. These are the people who all of a sudden have found themselves "liberated" by the collapse of society. No longer do they have anyone around to tell them that it's not right to hurt that person, to steal that car, to rape that woman, or anything else for that matter.

There are certainly those people who seek out this kind of lifestyle who will not embrace this so called freedom, but they will just run with and let themselves go wild.

Meanwhile, there are other people who, by the grace of handfuls of pharmaceutical assistance, have been able to fight back their "demons" and maintain at least a remote bit of sanity. Either that, or they are so medicated they shuffle around as if they were zombies before this outbreak ever occurred. Now, imagine that these people are out there, without their Seroquel, Haldol, Zyprexa or any of a half a dozen other anti-psychotic medications. Remove their chemical restraints and what will they do? I think it would be easier to state what they will not do, and that is to behave like civilized beings.

At the same time, the human factor is the stupidity in people as well. Well, maybe not "stupid," but it sure as hell is the lack of common sense, even in those occasionally temporary instances. In the movies, someone leaves a gate unlocked, opens the wrong door, or makes too much noise. They are not doing these things because they know they are going to be killed because of it. They are simply doing these things out of a temporary lapse of common sense.

Unfortunately, I knew too many people before this stuff happened that lived in a state of a total lack of common sense. I have to admit, these people used to drive me insane long before the shit hit the fan. How some people were able to function in life before these zombies still amazes me.

This is just some of the stuff that makes up the human condition, and that is why I am not worried about the zombie factor as much as I am about the human factor. Sure, the zombies want to kill me, but I am already aware of that and am prepared for whatever they can bring my way. Humans are unpredictable, you never know what someone is truly capable of doing until it is quite possibly too late to reverse whatever foolish thing they have done.

That is why we have to be extremely careful about who we let in to our little realm, such as it is. We have good people here and if we screw that up because we let the wrong one in, and any one of us dies because of it, then we have failed. It is as simple as that.

Speaking of our good people, I would eventually like to tell you more about each one of them, just so you can know who they were, how they lived and regretfully how some of them died.

Look, I am not a pessimist, I am actually just a realist. While I may be feeling "good" about things right now, and may be thinking we might actually make it through these dark times, I also know that we may not make it any longer than anyone else out there.

I have never been a betting man, and would not even attempt to wager on just how long any of us will make it. I do know this, though; with the great human beings that surround me right now, I just might be willing to become a betting man after all.

JUNE 7, 2009

It has been quiet over the past couple of weeks here at the camp. Even on some of our extended patrols we have seen more than a couple of zombies off in the distance. Like I said, it has been quiet.

We spotted a wisp of smoke off in the distance yesterday. From the amount of smoke it looks like it has the potential of being just one campfire, but it is difficult to tell. Our best guess is the camp is a few miles from here as the crow flies. We discussed it yesterday evening and we are planning on a scouting trip just to check them out. We have absolutely no plans of communicating with them at this time, we just need to find out who they are and if we can determine their intentions.

Taking the human factor into consideration we just don't want to walk up to them expecting them to be friendly. The chance we would be taking could be severely damaging to our party. Instead, we will be scouting them out from a distance and hopefully they will never even know we are there.

I will be going on this trip, along with Gabe and Wendy. I mentioned Gabe a few entries back but have not gotten around to introducing Wendy.

Wendy—what can I say about her other than she is a total surprise. Before this all started she worked at the Children's Museum in town, wrote in her free time, raised a beautiful family and practiced a vegetarian lifestyle. One of the things she only really mentioned a couple of times was that she had practiced the martial arts in the past. She even humbly stated that she had achieved her blue belt at one point in time.

Well, this chick is a warrior through and through. The tiny woman with the unassuming and endearing comic book voice is quickly becoming a legendary zombie slayer. Using a combination of her hands, feet and a five foot long white oak staff, she lays waste to everything in her path.

Honestly, it is a thing of pure beauty when she starts bringing that staff into action against the zombies. Like I said, it is white oak that she has wrapped leather cord around the end for about a foot down the shaft that helps her maintain a solid grip even when things are a little wet. The other end is a dark shade of brown that if you look closely enough, you can tell it is well stained with the coagulated blood of a handful of zombies.

She did not make the original journey out here with the rest of us; she told us she had a few things she needed to take care of before she could join us.

It was in the fifth week that Lars, I'll get to him in a little bit, came up to me and said "You're not going to believe who is working their way up the valley... Wendy!"

Sure enough, about an hour later she comes walking through the gates with her husband John and their daughter Fiona in tow. They didn't have much with them, and they looked a little rough around the edges, but they were finally here. She walked up to me, smiled and said, "I brought seeds!"

That's our Wendy.

Tomorrow morning we are going to head out and scout out this other group of survivors. My intention is to try to come in from the other side of their encampment as I feel this would sufficiently hide the direction of our camp if things go wrong. One of the last things I would want to happen is for them to follow our trail back here.

JUNE 12, 2009

Wow. I'm not even really sure where to start.

My last entry was 5 days ago. As I previously wrote, we were heading out to scout out the other encampment.

We found it with no problem, and honestly, I wish we had not. What we found there would have been unimaginable six months ago and to be quite frank with you, I am still reeling from finding something like this so soon.

Did I just write that? Am I really stating that if I witness what I just witnessed several years from now that it would be more acceptable? Why should it be more acceptable if it happens then and not now?

Jesus, there are times this new world sickens me.

What did we find out there? Fucking cannibals is what we found.

We are three or four months into the zombie apocalypse and these people have already turned to cannibalism?

Here we are, living off the land, eating wild game and livestock along with what is left of our stockpiled rations. There is still plenty of food out there if you are willing to look for it. Seriously, it is easier to find a cow than it is to find a living human these days.

Why would they do this?

When we finally found the camp, it looked like something out of your worst cannibalistic/apocalyptic nightmares. Skulls were on pikes all around the camp. Small piles of bones were scattered randomly about the area and there was even flesh hanging from ropes, drying in the open air like beef jerky.

I immediately thought of Wendy and wanted to get the fuck out of there for her sake. I looked at her and she had a single solitary tear running down her cheek. She looked at me and said, "This isn't right"

Gabe stepped in between us and dropped to a crouch while looking at the camp. He was shaking slightly and his jaw was moving, but he was chewing on nothing at all. He didn't even look at either of us when he popped up on one knee and said "This isn't fucking right... " then he launched out of our position and ran for the camp.

The primal roar tearing from his throat sounded like the legions of warriors from Valhalla. He ripped through the four men around the fire before I could even make my legs work enough to start running after him.

By the time I reached the heart of the camp it was done. The only living thing left was Gabe... and he was on his knees in front of the butchered body of a young woman.

They had been eating her.

He was covered in blood from head to toe other than where the tears from his eyes had mixed with and cleansed the blood from his cheeks.

This man that I have nothing but respect for stayed there on his knees, pulled me to his side and held on to my legs with all his strength, crying and repeating, "This isn't fucking right... this isn't fucking right... "

He could have needed hours, I don't know or care how long he needed, but I was going to give him all the time he needed. Eventually, he stood up and wiped the blood from his face and hands.

I swear to God, he looked in me the eyes and said, "Sorry dude."

Asshole.

We gathered all the weapons and ammo from around the camp while Wendy dumped gas on everything. While we gathered what we could, I found a pile of medical scrubs and a small pile of pill bottles under one of the shelters. Out of the dozen or so bottles, there were only three different names, and every one of the bottles were for psych meds. I caught up with Gabe and Wendy outside the camp, he lit the match and let it burn down to his fingertips before letting it drop, igniting the gas trail that led back into the campsite.

I made slight eye contact with him as he turned, and I'm not sure which fire burned hotter, the fire burning down this hellhole or the one in his soul.

It had taken us less than a day to get to that camp but it took us the last four to get back. We kept intentionally changing directions while trying to hide our trail, just in case there were more of them and they were trying to follow us. We never saw or heard anyone, we just needed to be cautious.

We were exhausted when we finally got back to camp. I seriously doubt Gabe or I slept on the trek back here. We didn't talk much on the way back, at least not to each other.

As a group we needed to talk about moving to another location, this one could have been easily compromised.

Thinking back to the other camp, there were more carcasses there than four people could have consumed. There was bedding and other supplies for a total of five, maybe six people in total. It is possible there are more people out there, were they out collecting?

I do know they had a radio with a bigger antenna than the one we have. Is it possible they have been responding to calls for help? Or have they been sending out requests for help and killing anyone that responds?

I do know one thing, we have to move and we have to move now.

JUNE 30, 2009

Well, we made it here.

How long we will be able to stay at this location I don't really know, but we will stay as long as we can.

Where exactly is here? Well, of all places on the Oregon coast we could have chosen, we chose a recreation of Lewis and Clark's winter encampment. It has high, sturdy log walls, room for all of us and it even has some replica equipment that should be usable. It is also far enough outside of the main town of Astoria that we should not have many zombies to deal with. While we are surrounded by rural residential areas, I doubt very highly there will be enough of a zombie population to cause us any real problems.

If nothing else, it will give us some respite from the past few weeks. Yeah you read that right, weeks.

After the cannibals, we did decide to move our camp and started the necessary work. We had secured vehicles at the bottom of the valley so we started dismantling the camp and moving our equipment into a central location for the long hike down.

On the third day we finally got there with the first load, and we left a small group of people behind to guard the gear and get it loaded up. Wendy and her family along with my wife Heather and our good friends Derek and Brenda were the ones to stay.

Those two, Derek and Brenda, were not doing too well without their medications and I knew it would not be long before I needed to get into a pharmacy for them. As of right now it is not very high on my list of things I want to do before I die, but I promised them I would do everything in my power to take care of them.

Hey, I'm not going to leave my favorite podcaster to the zombies, man!

Anyway, long story short, it took us a few more days to get everything else down to the vehicles and ready to move.

At one point in time we realized we had more people than room in the vehicles. I was trying to figure out what had happened when Wendy smiled at me and reminded me, "We walked here."

I just looked at her with what I can only guess was profound bewilderment at the realization that she and her family had walked all the way from Portland to be with us. I did all I could do at that moment, I hugged her and started to cry.

We unloaded some of the unessential stuff to make room for Wendy and her precious little family and then we headed west. We had decided to try heading to the coast, doing the whole water to our back thing.

To be honest with you, I just wanted to get away from this location. We could have headed east and I would have been just as happy.

One thing you need to realize about our group is that before the world was turned upside down, we could never even decide where to have our meetings. Let alone agree on a new location to set up a home base.

Fact is, the closer we got to Seaside, the more people were deciding that they did not like the idea of the coast. We stopped our vehicles in the middle of the crossroads of Highway 26 and 101, arguing about where to go and what to do when Fiona, Wendy's daughter pulled on my pant leg and said, "What about the fort?"

Lars asked, "Fort Stevens?"

She said "No, Fort Clatsop, we went there about six months ago."

Everybody kind of laughed at first but then we started talking about it and said why the hell not? As has been proven by our current situation, if it winds up being a bad idea, we will just move to another location.

So, here we are at Fort Clatsop for our brave last stand against the zombies, at least for now.

Now then, where is Sacagawea?

JULY 8, 2009

We have been here at the fort for just a little over a week now, and we have to admit, things are actually going well.

Wendy and John have taken to building a nice garden just outside the main gate, and Gabe and Lars have been working to expand the gate in order to encompass the garden.

Harley has gotten his radio set back up, and he even picked up a couple of people just last night. From what we could tell due to the strength of the signal, they were most likely on fishing boats off shore somewhere. They were two very distinctly different signals at different times, so there was no concern of it being one group trying to throw us off.

To be honest with you, they both sounded like they have completely lost it to me. One of them just kept repeating to himself, "I'm here... I'm here... " which told me he had been out there for far too long and it would be next to impossible to talk him in. The other one kept talking to someone in the background that I really don't think was there.

Harley was ready to tell him where we are when Gabe took the mic from him, then turned around and said something nobody else heard. The guy on the other end started screaming like a fucking maniac.

Gabe just put the mic down and started walking away. I asked him what the hell he said. His response? "Just pushed a pawn man, just pushed a pawn." So far today we have not been able to pick up their signals again.

Heather (my wife) and Emily (Lars' wife) have been taking care of Derek and Brenda as they got sick a couple days after getting here. I really need to make a med run for these two. Not only do they need stuff, but we are out of antibiotics and could use some other meds just in case.

Harley has volunteered to go with me down to Seaside to hit a pharmacy. He is good in a fight and he thinks quickly on his feet, which are both attributes I like in someone who will be watching my back.

We have been unable to decide where to go on the run. There is a small Coast Guard station close by, but there might still be active duty types there. We are not really sure we want to mess around with that scenario yet.

Astoria is the biggest town on the northern coast. It is also the closest town to us and sure to have a well equipped pharmacy, but like I just said... it is also the biggest town on the coast. A bigger town typically means a bigger zombie horde.

We are leaning more towards Seaside. It's more of a tourist location with fewer full time residents, and tourist towns mean fewer zombies. We also know that for a fact because we just drove through the town not that long ago. Even as quickly as we shot through Seaside, we only saw a couple of zombies.

Yeah sure, there is the Costco in Warrenton but we have our rule about Costco's. It's pretty much the same rule we have for Wal-Marts and gun stores. That rule is: STAY THE FUCK AWAY!!!

Every yahoo and their brother decided those were the type of places to go when the shit really started to hit the fan. You are either going to have some guy barricaded in the building, or more damn zombies than you can shake a stick at.

Sorry Gabe, I just can't shake that phrase.

Gabe used to joke about how many zombies it would take before you could no longer physically shake a stick at them.

Either way, at this point in time, we do not feel we have the firepower to attempt taking a Costco.

With that in mind, it looks like we will be taking a road trip to Seaside.

Harley and I need to get some rest. We could be in for a rough day tomorrow.

JULY 9, 2009

You know, there are certainly a few things that are missed from the days Before Zombies, like new zombie movies. Nobody is making those any more, and I have to admit, I doubt I would really be wanting to watch them these days. All I really need to do these days if I want to see zombies is just look out the window.

Now, Dutch Brothers coffee... oh man, what I wouldn't give for an ER-911 right now. BZ, this drink was like ambrosia man, six shots of espresso and Irish Cream flavoring... oh baby.

I can't forget peanut butter cups. Okay, yeah, I was a Chef so I'm sure I could make something like them, but it would never be the same. I did see a box of peanut butter cups with my name on it in the drug store but, well, I will get to that story in a moment. For now, just know... fucking zombies!

And one of the most important things missed from BZ, an easy trip to the store.

If you woke up in the middle of the night, sneezing, coughing, aching and needed some NyQuil? Well, all you had to do was climb in the car and go get it.

Even looking back at all those years that Heather and I did not have a car and rode the bus, it wasn't that hard. Simply plan with your bus schedule, be the master of your own timing and voila, you got your NyQuil.

Well, this is no longer BZ, and the buses aren't running anymore.

The zombies in Seaside were running though. Seriously, running as fast as we could.

What the hell? None of us have seen anything but shamblers until this horde today.

Why were they running? How were they running? And how the hell are they able to run so fast?

Harley and I had geared up, made sure the gas tank on the truck was filled, spare gas cans were placed in the rear and we hit the road. Seaside was only about 10 miles away, so this should have been an easy med run.

We pulled into the northern end of Seaside and stopped. No sign of zombies.

We continued to drive down the 101 to the RiteAid on the east side of the road, and stopped the truck close to the doors. We sat in the truck for about an hour, just waiting, listening and looking for signs of the undead. Nothing.

Harley broke the silence and asked me if I was ready.

I gave him my stock answer of, "No, but let's do this!"

We entered the store through the broken doors. I took the left side of the pie while Harley took the right. We stood there about 5 minutes, scanning with our weapon lights, listening and looking. Nothing.

Harley elbowed me gently and nodded towards the rear of the store, "Meds."

We cleared every aisle very carefully taking a good twenty minutes just to get to the actual pharmacy.

We hopped the counter and started filling our bags with everything we could get our hands on: broad spectrum antibiotics, inhalers, steroids, antidepressants, decongestants, you name it, we grabbed it. Harley even smiled at me as he dropped a bottle of Viagra in his bag.

Seriously? Viagra?

We were as loaded up as we needed to be and we were about ready to leave when Harley motioned at the safe.

"Narc's?"

Sure, why not? He pulled out what we are calling his mjolinir, which is nothing more than a 20-pound sledgehammer with a shortened handle and named after Thor's hammer. Even as wiry as Harley is, I still don't know how he can swing that thing like he does.

He took one swipe at the locking mechanism and basically knocked it back into the safe.

He just smiled as he started pulling out bottles of vicodin, percocet, morphine, demerol. Shit, no wonder he was smiling, he was the new pusher-man.

We were just climbing over the counter when it happened. A zombie came crashing through the door and closed the distance between the entry and Harley in no time flat.

Harley barely had the time to pull his arm back and let that hammer fly, slamming it into the zombies face.

Harley flew forward from the momentum of the hammer at the same time the zombie did this crazy backwards flip before landing on and breaking a rack of sunglasses.

I immediately went weapons up and started scanning the front of the store.

Harley got himself up and started laughing, asking me, "Did you see that shit?"

I said "Yeah, I saw that shit. I saw a running zombie!"

"Fuck! He *was* running, wasn't he?" He brought his weapon up and started scanning his side of the building just as another one hit the door.

I fired my AK and the zombie went down.

I called out to Harley, "Right!"

Harley called back, "Left!"

We each had our section of the pie and started to move towards the front of the building.

I fired, a zombie at my side of the entryway went down.

Two shots from my left, I can only assume two zombies went down.

Another shot from the left. Another zombie.

A scream came from my left and then something impacted hard into my body, knocking me to the side. I fell, rolled, and rapid fired a bunch of times into the chest of a zombie that had a fresh piece of meat in its mouth.

It fell back as I got to my knees, I dropped my AK, letting it hang from the sling, then I pulled my pistol and took that sucker's head off.

Harley was down, and he was bitten. Damn thing bit his hand and took his finger off.

Keeping my pistol in my left hand, I pulled my bolo from the sheath with my left, and as I fell to my knees at his side I swung the blade down at his wrist as hard as I could. I wish I could say it was a clean cut, but it severed the hand. I pulled the tourniquet out of his left chest pocket, we all keep one there just in case, and applied it to the wrist while we both did our best to keep our eyes open. Looking back on taking his hand off, I guess I did the right thing. Only time will tell.

With the tourniquet around the wrist, I pulled him up with me as I stood, his good arm around my neck, and just in time to see another zombie at the door.

This one was a freaking cheerleader! I am not kidding you.

Harley let out a strained laugh and said, "You wondered why I grabbed the Viagra!"

You have to love the spirit of this kid.

I hit her one time with a round from my revolver and she went down.

Sliding the revolver back into my holster, I transitioned back to my AK and started dragging Harley to the door.

We finally got to the truck, and I shoved him across the seat and got in just in time for a zombie to slam into the door as I was closing it.

We started to drive away as quickly as we could but I saw more of them in the rear view mirror.

God, my mind was working a million miles an hour. I told Harley to take some pills, while looking at the zombies in the mirror, and trying to stay on the road and put some distance behind us.

Harley said that we could not lead them back to the fort, that we needed to take them out then and there. I agreed that would be the biggest mistake we have made yet. Harley took his AR and slid it out the window, resting the hand-guard in the side view mirror.

I nailed a shaky power slide with the truck and we found ourselves facing the horde. Harley started firing and I punched the gas. What he didn't shoot, I nailed with the corners of the truck.

After about 5 minutes of this morbid demolition derby we finally got the last one and we hauled ass out of town. About 5 miles out I pulled off to the side of the road at an old produce stand. I jumped out of the truck, scanned the area and took out a zombie through the window, not wanting to risk the zed being able to get out of the building while I was taking care of Harley. I busted up some produce crates and got a fire going before I placed a shovel I had found into the fire.

By this time, Harley was pretty well doped up and was agreeable to just about anything. As I pulled him out of the truck I asked him what had happened, how the zombie had gotten him?

The little shithead grinned at me and said, "I was grabbing a Reese's cup for you"

Oh yeah, that's just what I need—guilt!

I led him over to the fire and sat him down while telling him the plan, then I asked him if he was ready.

The look in his eyes was a cross of the effects of the morphine he ingested and just a touch of insanity. "Hell, yeah! Let's do this!"

I pulled the shovel out of the flames by the handle and cauterized his stump. No matter, how much dope you put in your system, there is still nothing like the smell and sound of your own burning flesh to sober you up. There was nothing cowardly about the scream that escaped his lips. He didn't do anything I would not expect from anyone in that situation.

Once I got us back to the fort I got my medical kits together and performed a proper battlefield amputation. I like this kid, and I did the best I could with what I had to work with, so I really hope it works.

For now? I could use some sleep.

JULY 18, 2009

It has been somewhere around a week since the ill-fated med run. I have been losing track of the time and I have found that issue to not really be that bothersome.

I was always so conscientious about time BZ, always so prompt. Now I'm not even sure what day it is without looking at this journal and would not be able to tell you how long this stuff has been going on.

Maybe it just doesn't matter anymore. I know that none of us bother with watches anymore, that level of time has become completely irrelevant. No longer are we worried about that pesky doctors appointment or what time the next blockbuster movie is playing at the local cinema. If we really need to know the time, a quick look at the sun will get us as close to a time as we need to be.

I digress, so let me talk about Harley... what can I say about Harley? Well, a week ago he was bitten by a zombie, had a traumatic amputation of the left hand and third degree burns to the stump. That would have taken most people completely out of the game, but that was only the beginning for Harley. All of that trauma was followed by a less than sterile amputation at the wrist by someone who had never done the procedure, and yet today, the kid had the energy to yell at someone for turning a knob on his radio.

I would have to say Harley is going to be okay. I have pumped as much broad spectrum antibiotics into him as I felt he could safely handle and have been monitoring him constantly for signs and symptoms of infection. To date, there has been no sign of infection and the wound is healing beautifully.

Now, you are probably wondering, was I monitoring him so closely because I truly wanted to watch him for infection, or because I felt the need to be there to put him down if he turned?

You can take your pick. Either way, we got lucky this time.

Derek and Brenda are both doing much better now that they have some meds in them. She still has pains but with her rheumatoid arthritis that is to be expected. That doesn't heal like a cut or even a broken bone will after enough time. It's like bad luggage, once you have it, it is not going anywhere.

Derek is up and doing great. He is doing more around the fort to be helpful, at least more than he was able to when we were up in the woods. Here, he is helping out with day to day things along with doing some cooking, and he is even helping with the gardening.

There are definitely times I feel bad for these two. I can't necessarily say that a zombie world is a good place for vegetarians. So much of the food that vegans and vegetarians eat is organic or processed in other ways that eating "on the run" can be quite difficult.

Although, this is one that certainly has caught me by surprise... they are now eating mushrooms. These two people HATED mushrooms. Imagine that, a picky vegetarian. While they are eating them, it is not necessarily because they like them, but simply because they are available.

That is one of the nice things about being here in the Oregon woods; it is mushroom galore out here. For example, the queen of the forest—chanterelles—are all over the place. We have been picking them and handfuls of the other edible fungi of the forest every chance we get. To date we have had nobody poisoned by mushrooms, so my having been a chef is still having its benefits.

Back to Derek and Brenda...we love these two, we really do. It is kind of funny; we originally met because of his zombie movie podcast and quickly became friends.

Zombies... bringing people together even before they took over the world.

We started communicating with them on a daily basis when things started getting crazier by the way. He wanted to continue with his podcast to get the word out about the zombies, and up until the day I showed up at his door and told them it was time to go, he did exactly that. However, all good things must come to an end.

We had talked in the past that with their collective health issues they would not necessarily make it long in a PAW. So far we have found that to be true, and yet the fact is, they are going through changes and getting stronger and healthier. Hell, one might even go so far as to say the apocalypse has been good for them.

I will say this though, it has been of great assistance that they are surrounded by good people. Not just my wife and I, but every single one of us out here. With such a broad expanse of knowledge and capabilities, how can you not learn to adapt and survive?

Don't get me wrong, I was a big fat tub of shit with a bad heart, but I still had my strengths and those have been what have helped me. I have lost quite a bit of weight, all of us have, but I would have to say that we are all getting healthier in many regards.

Fort report. Wow, say that ten times fast.

The guys have been busy this past week. They have finished the wall around the garden and have been reinforcing the exterior walls. For the most part they were sturdy enough to hold back a zombie, they were just a little too short for our liking. While we have not seen any zombies climbing walls yet, it does not mean they are incapable of learning new tricks.

We have cut down a bunch of the timber from all around the fort and have been using that for the reinforcement. Seeing how that also gives us a little bit bigger kill zone around the perimeter, it has been a good call.

While using the timber for reinforcements we did something that we consider to be really smart. Instead of just building straight up, we angled the timber outwards. Nothing beyond forty-five degrees or anything like that, just enough that if anyone or anything were to try climbing the wall they would find that task to be just a bit more difficult than they could have hoped for.

We did have a nice surprise just a couple of days past. John, Wendy's husband, had noticed a black bear was digging around in our refuse pile. He quietly came back into the fort to let us know the bear was out there. Mr. Bear was still digging in the trash when we stepped back around the corner with our guns.

We have most of the meat salted and hanging to dry out. We did eat some great stew last night, and once the hide is tanned, somebody will have a nice blanket. We have to be like the Native Americans and use every bit of the animal we can use. We simply cannot afford to waste anything.

I remember reading that when Lewis and Clark were in this area 200 years ago, they killed something like a hundred plus elk during their winter stay. While we definitely do not have the herds like there used to be, this is still prime elk country. So when we set our minds to hunting down some elk, I doubt we will have much problem getting more meat.

Even Derek and Brenda have said they will likely partake in that. Their issue with eating meat is primarily whether the animal died cleanly or not. They just don't want to know the animal suffered. With that being said, they still were not too hot on the prospect of eating a bear. Considering the response Brenda had when she stepped around the corner and saw the animal hanging as we skinned it, I can understand. There is almost more than a passing resemblance between a skinned bear and a human being.

JULY 24, 2009

Over the past week I have started to notice something about Harley. He's getting stronger every day since the injury and subsequent treatment. That in itself should be good news, but I would not think he should be getting this much stronger.

It has to have something to do with the bite.

We all have seen plenty of zombie bites on a lot of zombie corpses, and you could almost always see where there was rapid tissue damage not just from the bite but from the infection. With Harley, I have seen no sign of infection around his stump, and not even anything I would have expected. There is NO sign of infection.

Yeah, I am a decent Corpsman, but shit, I am definitely no surgeon. Even with the antibiotics I loaded his system with I would have expected at least some signs of infection. Instead, what I am seeing is a wound that is healing far better than it should, and a patient who is doing far more than he should be able to do just a few weeks after losing a hand, let alone some things he should not be able to do, period.

I have talked to Derek and Heather about this and I have asked them both to help me by keeping their eyes on Harley. No, I did not tell them exactly why I want them watching him; I just want to know their observations.

To be honest with you, I don't even know if what I am thinking makes any sense. Maybe his recovery is normal and I am just too tuned into the possibility that it shouldn't be normal.

JULY 28, 2009

We got an elk!

Gabe was out on another one of his walkabouts; at least that's what I call them. He sometimes takes off for a few of days on his own. He always comes back but he never talks about it. I have tried many times to get him to talk to me about them, where he went, what he saw, you know, the typical stuff. He always just tells me he writes it down, and someday he will share those stories with me. He tends to walk away saying, "Until then, fuck off already!"

He has been gone for the past few days and when he came walking back up the trail we were just a little surprised to see him carrying the hind-quarter of an elk over his shoulder.

I opened the gate for him and asked, "Got an elk huh?"

"Yup."

That was basically the extent of the conversation.

I didn't want to ask him how he got it when he left his rifle behind and had nothing but his Nordic axe with him. I have to face the very real prospect that he took down an elk with nothing but his axe, and that fact is not too surprising.

Fortunately, he said he killed it less than a mile from here so a group of us all hiked out there to retrieve the rest of the elk. A Roosevelt Elk is a beautiful thing on the hoof, but a real bitch to drag through tall, wet grass. Now we have another hide to tan and plenty of work to do tonight and tomorrow getting the meat ready for preserving.

JULY, 2009
ENTRY BY GABE

Afternoon.

This is insane. I have been up in this damn tree for half a day now, why won't this elk leave? Okay, here is the situation, I am out here, hiking around, minding my own business, just collecting "my shit". Cole calls it a walkabout, and while that might be a better term for what I am doing out here, I refuse to call it that.

So here I am, walking through the grass when I come across what I initially thought was a small deer. I stood there looking at it for a moment when I heard this noise behind me. It turns out, it was not a small deer but a damned elk calf, and the noise behind me was the little critter's mother.

I took off running for the closest shoreline and climbed up this tree thinking it will get bored with me and go away, and I would be able to climb down from here. That was a good twelve hours ago. No matter what I throw at the elk, it just will not leave!

Evening

The elk is still there, circling the tree. I have consigned myself to the unfortunate situation of having to sleep in this tree. Using the rope I had in my pack I have secured myself in the tree and I am quite certain that barring something knocking the tree down, I will not fall.

Morning

She is still here at the base of the tree. The stupid cow has actually laid down at the base of the tree, wrapping herself around the trunk.

I have looked at all possible directions out of this tree and there is no way I can get out of here without her knowing I am on the move. I cannot outrun her and even though she does not have a massive rack of antlers, she has hooves which would tear me apart if she gets me down on the ground.

I think I am only about a mile from the camp but there is no way they could hear me. If I had not left the damn rifle behind for this walk, I would have been back home at the fort by now. Instead, I am fast approaching my second day in this damn tree.

Evening

Around noon I hit my breaking point, I couldn't take it anymore, I had to do something. She was back on her feet, walking in circles around the tree. So, about an hour ago, I pulled my axe and perched in the tree, waiting for the right moment. I let her go around a couple of times to make sure my timing was right. She stepped into my sight, I dropped from the tree and used the last of my strength to bring my axe to bear on the back of her neck.

I guess I hit her in the right spot and while I did not go as deep as I hoped, I went deep enough to sever the spinal cord. She hit the ground a split second after I did. Once I gathered my composure I did a quick field dress on her and brought a hind-quarter back to the fort this afternoon.

Lucky for me, nobody asked me how I got it. Good. Being stuck in a tree for a day is not exactly a story I want repeated.

AUGUST 22, 2009

It has been kind of quiet recently, which has been nice if I am to be completely honest. Even the briefest of respite in a land of the dead is welcome.

Even with the peace and little bit of relaxation here and there we have been working on the fort, even to the point of having extended outward, adding a little more space for us to spread outward. Space... yeah, even with so few humans around, space is still precious.

I should give a quick status check on everyone.

Heather is doing okay. Health wise she is still getting healthier. Mentally? She's doing really well. All of my bullshit talk back BZ must have done a better job of getting her ready for this stuff than I thought it did. To be honest with you, she's kind of thriving in more ways than one.

Derek and Brenda are doing well. The meds are holding up and that's good, but it is looking like we will have to hit a library sometime soon. They are running out of books and that is a priority for them, a priority I will be happy to oblige once we are secure enough here for the winter.

We have raided the visitors center here of everything they had, but how many different versions of the Lewis and Clark journals can someone read?

Lars and his wife Emily seem to be doing well. They could be better but who couldn't be? I have to admit, Lars is kind of quiet and does not talk much to anyone other than Emily and Harley. He and I used to talk all the time when we worked together, but these days, especially more recently, he is very limited on conversation. Emily is as healthy of a specimen as one could ask for. She was a grade school teacher before the dead rose and pretty much worked out, ran several miles a day and led a fairly standard life. While I am sure these two miss some of the creature comforts of day to day life, they are, by all outward appearances, doing fine.

Gabe has been gone for most of the past week on another walkabout. This time he did at least take one of the replica Model 1792's from the visitor center and the powder and lead balls they had on hand. He is quite the image with an old flintlock rifle, Nordic axe and the bearskin that he claimed and turned into a poncho. I can't tell, is he more of a Viking or is he slowly turning into a mountain man?

Wendy and her family are doing wonderfully. Most of their time is taken up gardening and writing in their own journals. She has also become a master mushroom hunter, spending almost two hours a day just hunting for clusters of fungi.

Harley is continuing to dazzle me. His incision has completely healed to the point that you cannot even see a scar. He has a perfectly healed stump. It is medically fascinating and if the shit was not smeared all over the wall after taking a run through the fan, I would have him before a half dozen medical boards for examination. To date he is not showing any other signs of physical change so it is unlikely that the virus is taking its own sweet time in killing him. In fact, it is nothing like that at all. He is getting better every day, and not just physically better from the injury, but better in all regards.

For example, just last week I watched him sprint across a clear cut that was a good two-hundred yards across. As far as I know, he didn't know I was there because I could see him looking around to make sure nobody was watching before he took off. Honestly, the last time I saw something move like that was the zombies at the pharmacy.

What did kind of freak me out was that once he reached the other side of the cut, the wind changed and blew from behind me. His head snapped and he looked right at me. I was 200 yards away and watching him with a pair of binoculars. He was sniffing at the air as I looked at him. A crazy little smile spread across his face and then he turned around and disappeared into the tree-line.

Back in camp he has been talking to someone, a young lady that says she is trapped in her family's house and is using her father's radio. She says her dad is still in the house, she can hear him. Harley keeps trying to get a location on her without letting her know where we are, but she keeps ignoring the question. We have to assume that she has either completely lost it or she is lying to him.

To date there has been no word from Lenny. It has been many weeks since he left and we have to account for the fact that we have moved since then. Before we left the original camp we left a fairly cryptic message letting him know we were heading for the coast. Even if he were to head west to the ocean, he would be unable to determine whether we had headed north or south.

Truth is, as much as I hate to admit this, I doubt we will ever see him again.

Jesus, how can I forget this? We heard a helicopter a couple of days ago.

With us being so deep in the trees we could not make out a distance or direction that it was flying, but it was a helicopter, and it raised a hell of a commotion in the fort.

Who are they? Where are they from? Do we want to find out?

Yeah, that's a triple case of I don't know, but I sure would like to find out.

AUGUST 29, 2009

We finally talked to the girl Harley has been communicating with. Harley had her on the line last night and she was finally answering the right questions, and giving the right answers. I have to be honest with you, I was skeptical, but we all talked about it and took a vote with the results being a rescue op this morning by Harley and Lars.

Why was I so skeptical? Well, we have this young woman, twenty-something, who has been using her father's complex radio, keeping the batteries replaced/recharged, and she has survived months with little to no food or water. Add in the fact that her father is supposedly shuffling around in the house just the other side of the door. It didn't sound right to me, but the boys are capable of taking care of themselves. If nothing else, I think they just wanted an excuse to get out and do something.

We did agree on one thing before they left the fort. If they get there and it is a bad scene, and they are able to escape, then they are not to come straight back here. At least not right away. The last thing we need is someone coming to the fort and challenging us for what we have claimed.

Well, that is apparently all moot. Her name is Julie, she is 19 years old and she is not only incredibly malnourished, but has also suffered more than any 19 year old should. All of the girls in the fort took her back to our bathing area and helped her get cleaned up and into some fresh clothes. Needless to say, we will be burning her old clothes on the refuse pile the next burn day.

I talked to Harley and Lars as soon as they got back, and everything went like clockwork. They got there, found a few zombies outside of the house that they easily dispatched, and then moved into the house.

Julie had given them a verbal layout of the house and was able to tell them where her father was most likely going to be. They removed him from the equation and while Lars dragged his body outside and under the stairs, Harley talked her out of the room she had locked herself in. Even knowing they were coming for her, and the fact they were speaking to her, she was still hesitant to open the door. She finally opened the door and they got out of the area.

They did make one mistake on the way back when they took a wrong turn and shot right past the fort. They wound up getting a little closer to Astoria than we had been planning on when they pulled onto 101 just before the bridge. What they saw on the bridge is what really disturbs me and everyone else here.

They said there were a bunch of slow movers on the bridge into the city. No big deal, that is to be expected. However, Lars reported seeing something moving fairly fast across the bridge. They thought maybe it was a survivor that had seen them and was making a run for it.

They did exactly what they should have done, only one of them got out of the truck, weapon at the ready and waited. They were far enough away from the horde so they were in no immediate danger, but they were coming. They were coming slowly, yes, but still coming towards them. Then the survivor made his way over a car, and that was when Lars said he started to sweat. It was the realization that your typical survivor would not have the speed or stamina to do what this one was doing.

Apparently Harley started saying to shoot, over and over. Since it was still half a football field away Lars did a quick double tap with his AR, hitting it in the torso just to try to slow it down. It didn't just slow down, it went down, and it stayed down. They made the right choice of getting out of there and heading back to the fort as quickly as possible. There were too many zombies for them to have made their way to the one they had just shot to verify it was not a survivor. From everything they told me, and since Harley knows what the fast movers look and move like, I have no reason to believe it was anything but a zombie.

I don't know about you, but I find that to be downright fascinating. As far as it going down the way it did, there may well be a simple explanation: it is entirely possible that he had a one in a million shot and severed the spinal cord.

While that would explain it hitting the deck like it did, it is also highly unlikely that the shot was that lucky.

When Harley and I did the med run and had our run in with the fast movers, we were hitting head-shots at close range, but never took the chance of a torso shot. It is possible that for whatever reason, the fast zombies do not need a head shot to permanently put them down. That would be very interesting indeed. I think I would like to get my hands on one of these new zombies.

SEPTEMBER 3, 2009

Julie is doing better than I would have expected. Even though she has only been with us for about 4 days, she has been taking in nourishment from day one and that is a good sign that she should bounce back just fine. You have to love the resilience of the younger people. If it had been an older person stuck in that house like she had been for as long as she was, we would likely be digging a grave by now.

Harley has been at her side almost constantly since she arrived, and while he is kind of shirking his duties around the fort, Lars has stepped up and is helping to man the radio and other tasks Harley usually performs. Honestly, we are not so strict here that any of us are holding it against Harley, right now he needs to do what he needs to do and we are all fine with it.

During their debriefing, Lars told us that there was a mini-mart that they had passed when retrieving Julie. They both said it looked to be intact and Lars asked for a volunteer to go back and hit it with him.

Derek stepped up and said he would love to get out and do something to help out. Good on you Derek, I knew this whole PAW thing would be good for him. I sent my shotgun with him and he also took one of Heather's machetes. He laughed and asked where his first aid kit and adrenaline shot was. That got quite a laugh from most everyone in the fort. We are no longer just playing Left 4 Dead on Friday nights, we are living it on a daily basis these days.

Fortunately, for all of us, they had a relatively uneventful trip. They reported that there were only a couple of zombies outside the mart, and just one on the inside. From what they said, the doors were all locked and barricaded from the inside. This tells me that someone got bit early on, locked themselves inside the mini-mart and later died.

They did get some good provisions including a lot of canned goods, some alcohol, and quite a bit of bottled water. While they brought back a truckload, they say there is more stuff than they could grab so it looks like we will be making another trip out there tomorrow.

For the record, Gabe has been gone on his latest walkabout for nine days now. Wherever you are brother, stay strong.

SEPTEMBER 4, 2009

We got one of the fast moving zombies, we actually got one. Unfortunately, I am even more baffled now that we have one.

Lars, Heather and I went back to the mini-mart to grab the rest of the provisions. Heather was acting as sentry on top of the truck while Lars and I loaded the bed down with everything we could grab. We had not been there for long when Heather let out a loud "FUCK!"

We ran out to the truck to find her standing on the hood, pointing her AK towards a zombie trying to climb up the grill guard on the front. At first I thought he was just a short little shit, then I realized he didn't have legs. Heather was busy trying to tell us it was one of the fast zombies we had been looking for. She was convinced he had to be one as she said he was moving "way faster than any legless zombie I had ever seen!"

Now, seriously here, what kind of fucked up world is it that you can eventually compare the speeds of legless zombies? I can hear the conversation now, "Well, this legless bastard was way faster than that legless bastard!"

In an attempt to make a long story short, Lars and I made our move, he took the left side and I took the right side. We had this thing zip tied to the grill before it even knew what was happening. Fortunately, they held and we were able to get him back to the fort after cleaning out the mini-mart.

Here are my observations of Stumpy, as one of the girls called him, so far and, well, as I stated previously, I am even more baffled now.

1. He lost his legs traumatically, whether they were chewed off back in the beginning and that was what turned him, or they were lost due to a vehicle mishap, I really am unable to tell. However, what I am seeing is that there are signs of healing in the wounds. My eyes did not want to believe it either when I first noticed it, but no shit, his wounds are actually healing.

2. Along with the signs of healing taking place on the stumps of his legs, there are calluses on the palms of his hands. For being a zombie dragging himself around like it has been for several months, you would think there would be no tissue left on its hands, let alone to actually show signs of calluses.

3. There is a definite pulse, even if it is going so fast I was hardly able to detect it. How is there a pulse? Is this something new or have the zombies always had a pulse? I had my hands around the throat of a zombie back at the beginning and there was no sign of a pulse. The blood should be congealed and fairly solid in the veins, it is the reason why they do not explode into a wet mess like you see them do in the movies. How is it possible that there is a pulse? I cut into his arm to see what happened. It did not respond to the cut, and the incision itself bled, but it was not blood. Fact is, it looks more like straight plasma more than anything else. I don't remember the colors from my first interaction with the Snyders (That's what Derek has started calling them, in reference to the director of a movie from 2004 featuring the faster zombies). I was a little too preoccupied with the fight to be wondering what color of liquid they were bleeding, and Harley said he paid no attention to any possible bleeding either.

4. Stumpy still wants to eat our flesh. It pulls so hard against its restraints that we can hear bones creaking and muscles tearing. We replaced the zip ties with handcuffs just to make sure he would not be able to break loose.

So, with the little bit of extra knowledge we were able to acquire, what does this leave us with? We have zombies that are slow moving, they want to eat our flesh, and they are destroyed with a head-shot. Now, we also have zombies that are faster and stronger than we are, and while they still want to treat us like a double cheeseburger, they can apparently die from any traumatic injury that would take down a normal human being.

Even though they appear to be easier to destroy, why do I still get the feeling we are fucked?

SEPTEMBER 8, 2009

We felt we had learned all we would be able to learn from Stumpy, so we dispatched it today and burnt the corpse on the refuse pile outside the fort. I had planned on simply putting a round in his skull but I was quickly out voted as most of the fort felt there was one more thing we could learn from him.

Lars brought out his 9mm pistol and shot it once in the right side of the chest, creating what would have been a sucking chest wound on a human. This injury did not even phase it, even though we stood there and watched it "bleed" for several minutes. John finally stepped up with a machete and pushed it between the ribs and into the heart, an injury that killed it immediately.

After we burned the corpse, everyone was in kind of a funky mood. While I am not sure if it was the final lesson Stumpy gave us or not, I know a few of us felt "dirty" for having let him hang there bleeding like that. No matter what he was now, at one point he had been a human being.

Fiona stepped up to me as I sat at the table and told me that she has been reading about how Lewis and Clark got their salt by boiling seawater in brass cairns down the coast. She was just wanting to know if we could get our salt that way as well. While we have plenty of salt for now, we told her that when the time comes, we will make a trip down there and show her how it is done.

You have to love the resiliency of children. The world is collapsing all around us and this bright little girl still has the desire to learn. Sure, we all recognize that the chances of her learning how to fly a plane or program a computer someday are getting slimmer by the day, but there is still plenty to learn.

She

Helicopter!

SEPTEMBER 15, 2009

So, we heard another helicopter. Problem is, it's not a chopper. It was a Reaper, the second generation drone like the Predator. These things are flown remotely by someone in a nice cozy bunker someplace. What this means for us is that there is still someone in operation, and they are someplace close.

Where could they be though? Camp Rilea is the closest military base of any substantial size. There is the Coast Guard station close to us that has an airstrip but we haven't seen anything moving over there. Add in the fact that each time we have heard this thing, it was already in full flight. If it were taking off from close by, we would have heard the sound earlier than we did.

All that we know for now is that it flew from south-southwest of our location and it was headed to the north-northeast. We could just barely make it out through the trees, but we were able to determine it could not have been more than half a mile from us.

Harley was already running towards it by the time I got outside the fort walls, and as I have documented before, the guy can really run these days. If I remember correctly he was a track and field star back in high school, but these days it is totally different. He hauls ass across rough terrain just like the Snyders are capable of doing.

He was able to at least get close enough to be able to use his binoculars and make out what he said were crop sprayers protruding from beneath the wings. Not wanting to be sighted or potentially sprayed with anything, he ran back to the fort and reported his observations.

This just keeps getting better all the time. Not only do we have a plethora of zombies to worry about, now we have black government drones flying around spraying god only knows what.

God... Yeah. He checked out a while back, didn't he?

SEPTEMBER 18, 2009

We have decided to move into Astoria. Well not MOVE into Astoria, but venture into Astoria for supplies. I lived in Seaside—which is ten miles or so south—for a couple of winters during my childhood, so I have a very good idea of the lay of the land.

I know right where a sporting goods store is that has a gun shop in the basement, and I also know right where the library is. While that is all well and good, we are a touch over 7 miles from them both under ideal conditions.

With the bridge into town having more zombies on it than we want to go through, we figured this plan will be our best shot. We plan to take out as many as we can from a distance and then pull back, allowing them to potentially repopulate the bridge, then repeat the process. While this may not seem like an ideal plan, we figure this will give more zombies from in the town to make their way onto the bridge. I would rather have to deal with them in a narrow killing zone than to have them have any semblance of a home court advantage.

Our first day out we took out well over a hundred of them. While it is definitely morose work, we actually kind of had fun doing it, but mostly because of what we were using. Harley and I had both of our old Mosin Nagant 91/30's while Lars pulled his 98k Mauser out of the weapons locker.

So here we were, 3 zombie hunters laying waste to a bunch of zombies on a bridge at distances of 100 to 400 yards using World War II weaponry. Sure, it would be better if we had an armored personnel carrier that was properly armed, but these old warhorses have worked just fine.

So far our plan has worked, and for the last two days we have been going back to find the bridge re-populated with zombies. Why can't they hit the waterfront or something? Why the hell are they on the bridge? Oh well.

I keep thinking that with a couple more days of this and we will be out of ammo for these weapons. Hopefully it will be enough.

SEPTEMBER 22, 2009

It may have taken us longer than we had initially hoped, but finally, after another three days, the bridge is clear to the point that we felt good about crossing it.

Harley decided to stay back at the fort. With Julie still in recovery mode he feels he can do more good there than he can on this trip. Considering his current "condition", I felt okay leaving him behind basically by himself. While Emily is getting better with her shooting, she is still not on par with most of us, so we had her stay behind to help out Harley.

With that being said, the trip went smoothly and I, for one, feel good about it being a quick trip.

Our post bridge plan was that we would drop Lars and Derek off on the main strip to hit the gun store, while Brenda and I would hit the library.

Why the library? Morale!

Some fresh books would be great back at the fort and besides, I know what it would mean to Derek and Brenda. Since they are out here because of me, I felt I owed it to them. Okay, yes, they would be dead by now if it were not for the rest of us, but since I chose to make them my responsibility, I will do what I need to do in order to look after their welfare.

Heather opted to drive the truck with Brenda in the cab while Derek, Lars and I were in the bed. Derek was facing the rear with my shotgun, while Lars and I swept the road ahead and to the sides.

Going over the bridge was a little sloppy at first. The tires kept spinning on all the zombies we had taken out over the past few days, and it took Heather a little while to get used to the feeling. Once we got about halfway across it was pretty clear driving and what few zombies were left, Heather opted to just drive right over . This was a decision that made for a stinky, wet, nasty, gut drenched ride in the back of the truck. That's okay, she's the one that has to sleep next to me tonight when I am not on watch.

We got into town and were not seeing any major hordes of zombies. This proved that we had made the right decision to do the work on the bridge before moving into town. Still, I was surprised that there were not as many zombies as I might have expected.

We also saw no signs of survivors anywhere. No sheets, flags, sheets of plywood with painted messages, nothing. Even in a town this size, I would have expected to have seen someone that was making a stand someplace in town.

I directed Heather to the gun store first as it was on the main stretch. I had already drawn a map based on my memories to Lars and Derek, so as long as there were no major changes inside the store, they would know right where to go.

They hopped right off the truck and took up their positions at the entry way and started a proper entry. Moments later I saw them disappear down the stairs around the corner.

According to Derek they only came across a couple of zombies, but they had a hell of a time getting into the gun store itself. The doors were heavily barricaded from the inside. Once they got through they found what I can only assume was Sky, the gunsmith and owner of the shop. Derek tells me the corpse was sitting in a chair in the middle of the area, guns in a state of readiness were all over the counters, empty MRE pouches and dehydrated meal packs were all over the place. It sounds like Sky took a last stand in his shop. He probably starved to death months ago.

They did get some good items, basically grabbing every weapon that accepted the ammo they were able to find. We had decided a long time ago, there was no real sense in taking weapons we can't shoot.

Brenda and I were unsurprisingly lucky when Heather dropped us off at the library. It was unlocked and there was not a single zombie inside the building. There were just a few shambling around on the outside, and they were easily taken down. I cleared the way with my machete, figuring there is no reason in ringing the dinner bell when there is no real reason to do so.

There was one zombie there that was acting funny. Funny as in, it just sat there, on the top step, growling and hissing at us, but not making any attempt to get up and move towards either one of us.

Brenda saw the name tag first and said, "She's the head librarian," and then she just stood there looking at her for a moment. I was getting ready to say something when she drew her Ruger 22 pistol and put one in her eye socket. The instant the corpse fell over into the grass, Brenda started to cry.

I didn't bother asking her what the problem was, I could tell what was going on and figured it would be best to give her the moment she needed. Brenda is someone that has lived in or through books much of her life, both for education and entertainment. Basically, books mean a lot to her, as they did to the librarian. You don't become a librarian for the money or the fame. No, it is a job you take for the love of books. For Brenda, shooting the librarian must have been akin to shooting an old friend.

The tears were of respect, I knew that, and so did Brenda. When she was finally ready she wiped her eyes, took a deep cleansing breath and said "Let's go".

I told her to take more time if she needed it, I would continue standing watch. Besides, we still were not sure what was waiting for us inside, so if she needed to take a breather, she should continue to do so. She declined the need for more time, so in we went.

Like I said earlier, the library was clear. I went for reference books and she went about grabbing everything she could. Before I could even ask she yelled out, "No! I am not grabbing any PAW books!"

Long story short, we got out of town without a major fight of any kind. Everyone made it back without a scratch, at least none physical. We got what we were after and we have an idea of what to expect when we go back for more.

SEPTEMBER 26, 2009

We have been back into Astoria a few times since the first trip. For the most part we have been hitting the grocery store just the other side of the bridge and we have been able to make out with a ton of canned goods, bottled water, propane tanks, barbecue supplies, all sorts of things.

We have raided every gas station this side of town and actually wound up having to grab several more gas cans just to get everything we were able to take.

None of us have been able to get a feel for what happened here in Astoria. There is too much stuff left behind, there are way too many provisions in the stores, the gas stations still have a bunch of fuel left and the town actually looks good. It is almost like the townspeople up and disappeared shortly after the initial outbreak. Then again, maybe we should not look a gift horse in the mouth and be thankful to the citizens of Astoria for leaving us with fairly easy pickings.

Harley has been on the radio a lot lately, listening for anyone else in the area and there has not been a peep. He recently took Julie, Lars and Emily back to her house to grab more of her things and her dad's radio and antenna. Emily got a chance to show the boys how it is done and dispatched a couple of zombies at the house. It was just another quiet raid in a zombie infested world.

If not for a minor concern about potential raiders I would almost say we should clean out Astoria and reclaim it.

Where we are, though, is a good place. Sure we could use more room, but we would probably be complaining about space wherever we wind up.

I think it is something to consider eventually. We could take out the bridges, fortify barricades at either end of town, and have minimal worries. If we could add another ten good people to our outfit, I think we could do it.

For now, damn me, I keep eying that Costco at Warrenton. It's that prize that I know is going to get me killed, but a prize that I absolutely must have.

There would potentially be more food in there than we could eat in years. The clothing and bedding that is in there, the tents, the bicycles, almost everything we could ever ask for is in there waiting for us to come and take it.

I know we need to leave it alone. I'm not the only one that keeps thinking about it; we keep looking at each other and saying it, "Costco". Then we just kind of shake our heads and laugh about it. It is one of those things that we always said we would not do if the time ever came. There are too many risks, too many concerns.

Sure, they might be unfounded concerns, but go ahead and feel free to place a huge emphasis on "might."

We could also walk in there and have nobody or no thing contest us for it, or we could also be wiped out by an army, living or undead.

If we did it, we would have to be smart about it, and that is the biggest problem; there is nothing smart about it.

Right now we actually have a ton of food. We are even using the visitor center here at the fort for our food storage and it is damn near stacked floor to ceiling. There are only eleven of us, twelve when Gabe returns, and my experience as a chef tells me we have close to 6 months worth of easy food. Add the garden that is close to producing, along with the wild game we take occasionally, and we have enough food for a long time to come.

If we had a couple more really good people, and more firepower than we currently have, maybe we could do it. I guess the biggest question is, are we that greedy that we need to even consider it?

OCTOBER 8, 2009

We actually had a visitor here at the fort today, a real live human being.

I was in the back of the fort checking our supply of dried meat when I heard a sudden commotion from out front. I went running out and found Lars with his AR trained on a man on his knees, with his fingers interlaced on top of his head while Harley patted him down. Nice teamwork guys.

His name is Truman and he lives deeper in the woods than any of us have gone so far. I get the feeling he has been living out there for a lot longer than the outbreak. He said had only come down looking for a few supplies, a new sleeping bag, some boots and that's about it. He wasn't looking for food or water. Fact is, he was even hesitant to eat or drink much when we did offer it.

Truman told us that we were the first humans he has seen in months. I honestly think he was more scared of us than we were about what he could mean for us. There was something in his eyes though, a look I had seen a few times before. He struck me as a beaten man with nothing left to live for. He said he had no friends, he lived completely on his own and from what I could tell, he had nothing to care for. I have to wonder if we hadn't taken him for a zombie when he approached the camp and shot him, would that have been what he was looking for?

We gave him boots, fresh clothes, a new sleeping bag, and one of the handful of small tents we had grabbed from the sporting goods store. Brenda even brought out a book for him which he took with the slightest of smiles before simply turning and walking back in the direction he had come from.

As a group, we don't know if we will see Truman again or not, but if we do, we agreed that he will be welcome.

OCTOBER 11, 2009

I took a hike yesterday out to the Coast Guard station just to take a look from outside the perimeter. We had been by the airstrip several times and never seen anyone out there, but this was a trip I wanted to make by myself and as quietly as possible. Basically, I was looking to see if I could pick up on anyone hiding out or any other kind of covert activity.

We have spotted the drone a couple more times in recent days and it has to be coming from someplace close. Since this is the only part time military airstrip in the immediate area, I feel it has to be coming from here, even though we have not been able to hear anything taking off or landing here.

I found a good spot in a cluster of trees at the end of runway 31, secured myself into a fairly tall, yet sturdy tree, and proceeded to watch.

For the next 24 hours I looked at a couple of HH-65 Dolphins, a USCG Jetstream and a handful of civilian aircraft.

Funny... thinking that with all the research I did in school for a report on the functioning of helicopters I might just come back sometime and give it a try. I feel that I have the basic understanding, I just need some practice.

I saw a lot of birds and other wildlife all over the tarmac but nothing else. No zombies, no people, no drones. I saw nothing and heard nothing, not even the hum of a hidden generator that would potentially give away a bunker.

This place was dead.

This morning I lowered myself out of the tree, cut a hole in the fence and entered the airstrip. I made it all the way to the Coast Guard dispensary and still there was no sign of anyone, or anything. The door of the dispensary was locked so I loaded one of my door breaching rounds.

It was one of those rounds my wife gave me the stink eye for buying several years ago. Instead of shot, it has a load of aluminum powder encased in plastic. When fired directly at a lock, it expends all of the energy in the moment of impact. I tested them out back in the day and to be honest, it is quite impressive what it does to a lock.

I loaded one into my shotgun, looked around the area and then blew the locking mechanism out of the door, pumped another round into the chamber and stepped into the clinic.

I found the building to be clear. There were no zombies, and no humans.

There was no mess either, unlike a lot of the hospitals and clinics we had seen in the big city.

This looked like somebody had just locked the doors one day and left. The power was out and the electronic lock on the pharmacy door held tight and since I only had the one breaching round with me, I needed to find another way in. I stepped out into the patient waiting area and was happy to find the shutters were not closed at the pharmacy. All I needed to do was knock out the glass and climb in.

I grabbed everything relevant that would fit in my bag, stuck everything else that I wanted but was not able to take with me into a box and then slid it up into the false ceiling. I figured that in the unlikely event someone else would show up and hit the pharmacy before I am able to go back, they will think all the good stuff is gone and not think to look in the ceiling.

I got back to the fort just a little while ago, and yes I caught some shit for being gone so long. In my defense, I did tell them I would be gone overnight. At the same time, I am glad to find that they still worry about me.

OCTOBER 12, 2009

Fort Report

It has been a while since I talked about everyone, so how is everyone doing?

Heather, my wife, is doing well. She has continued to lose a lot of weight and has gotten stronger with every passing day. She stands watch just like anyone else and does the best she can to pull her weight around the fort. She helps with cleaning, teaching Fiona, food gathering, you know, whatever she can do.

What about the bad side? Well, I have caught her off crying by herself many times. She has been thinking about her mom more and more often. While she knows we made the right decision to not make our way cross country to try to get to her, she still has her moments of doubt. Her mom and her boyfriend refused to listen to us and got the flu vaccine anyway. A couple of days later she called them and they were both sick as hell. Ultimately, she knows what happened to them, she just doesn't like knowing that they are potentially among the walking dead.

Julie is doing much better than she was the first time we all met her. She is actually quite a lovely young lady, energetic, smart and is willing to learn what she can to help. She is becoming more proficient with firearms every day and Harley has been taking special care teaching her everything he can about the HAM radio and the portable solar panels we use to keep the batteries charged.

Harley is doing great. His physical prowess has apparently leveled off. His condition is no longer a secret these days, not since the time he ran after the drone. There were some definite questions from everyone after that happened.

Having it out in the open has helped me though, as we have been able to do more testing to see what exactly he is capable of.

1. He can pick up the back of the truck.

2. He can cover 100 yards in right around 10 seconds.

3. He has heightened senses; sight, smell, hearing

4. His pain threshold is through the roof. Basically, he feels no pain.

5. His regenerative capabilities are amazing.

No, his healing is nothing like a mutant, but a small cut heals in just a couple of days instead of a week or more. That is simply amazing.

One more thing about Harley, he has it bad for Julie. I can't really blame the guy, they are close in age, she is an absolute doll, and the feelings he is having for her are mutual.

Lars and Emily. They seem to have taken to spending more time away from most of us recently. It took me a little while to realize why they were staying away. In fact, the women in the fort had noticed it days before I did. She is apparently pregnant and I am certain they are simply trying to figure out how to handle things. Whatever the choice, it is theirs to make. I do know that I am glad the decision is not mine. The thought of bringing a child into this world in particular is not something I would even consider. Maybe someday when—or if—we are able to reclaim it from the zeds, then we can start thinking about repopulating the planet. Now is not the time though.

Derek and Brenda, those two are my shining stars. A funny thing happened on the way to the PAW... they have undergone significant changes and have turned into survivors. I don't remember the last time I saw Derek using his inhaler and that is something I don't want to jinx. He still has his back problems but they seem to be getting milder and the flare-ups are less frequent. As with all of us, he has lost a significant amount of weight and that has surely helped with the back and the breathing.

Brenda is doing great. I am not saying her arthritis is gone, that will never happen, but she is having fewer issues with it. She had a hell of a time when we first left the city, but she kept pushing herself through the rough spots. She made the decision that now is the time to stand up and live, and it is not the time to lie down and die.

They are both now significantly more proficient with firearms and have been able to move into using long guns a little more frequently than before. This makes me feel much better when we have to do something requiring the weapons. I look back to when we did our first Astoria raid, all Brenda had for weapons was a machete and a .22 revolver. She also had me, but if we had run into a horde, we would have been hosed.

Today she carries a pair of double action .357's, one on her right hip and one in a shoulder holster. Those are with her all the time and when we go out, she has a lever action rifle in .357 that she carries with her.

Derek is a fan of the blade and carries one with him at all times, but he still carries a 1911 on his hip with an AR as his preferred long gun.

Wendy, John and Fiona? Not much to say about this little family. Beautiful people, kind, compassionate, and GREEN THUMBS! Their garden is looking fantastic and even here late in the fall is still producing some winter produce, specifically potatoes. They have chosen to not teach Fiona how to shoot yet, and I respect that. They simply want to protect her from "that" aspect for as long as they can.

All we, as residents of the fort, have asked, is that Fiona be with an adult at all times, simply for her own protection. That has been an easy task as Heather and Fiona have latched on to each other something fierce as teacher and student. I know this much, Heather will never let anything or anyone get to Fiona, not without going through her first.

How am I doing? I feel that I am doing well. Sure, I am a little tired, but good for the most part. I have lost more weight, I am getting a lot more exercise, and I am eating healthier. I really can't complain.

There are plenty of times recently that I have stopped and thought about those that are not with us anymore. I wonder about my brother and his family, and I wonder about my daughter at times. Maybe it helps to lessen the pain that she estranged herself from me years ago, but I still wonder about her and miss her.

As for those of us from our small group that are missing:

It's been several months now since Lenny left. We can only assume that, well, I don't really want to assume anything. Speculating will get us nowhere.

Gabe? He took off several weeks ago and has not been seen since. All I can say is, God help anyone or anything that got in his way. There is nothing worse than fighting a man already engaged in battle with his own demons.

For now, the gates are closed, Lars is on watch, and Fort Clatsop is secure and well.

OCTOBER 13, 2009

A couple of us went back to the airstrip today, I wanted to grab the rest of the meds I stashed last time and I wanted to take a look around at some of the other buildings. I took Derek with me on this trip because I thought it would be good for him to get out of the fort and if I ran into anyone or anything this time, it would be nice to have some backup.

We quickly covered the mile, maybe mile and a half distance, and found my original hole in the fence, then headed towards the buildings. By the time we made it to the dispensary Derek was huffing and puffing a little bit and for the first time in weeks he had to use his inhaler. I just stood there, scanning the area until a sign on one of the closer buildings caught my eye. It was a small sign, but the words held large potential for us. The sign read USCG Security Office.

A USCG Security Office could potentially have a weapons locker.

We breached the door with me taking point on the entry. Even though Derek has been paying attention during all of our room clearing talks and exercises, I do not think he is quite ready to be taking point. We will be getting him fully up to speed sooner than later as we all want everyone to be able to do each others' jobs.

I never like to talk about this kind of stuff to these guys, but I want everyone to basically know what everyone else knows in case the inevitable finally happens. I could get taken out by a zombie tomorrow, and if that happens, then who would be their Doc? If Derek never learns how to clear a building, what is he going to do if he winds up being the last one standing?

With that being said, he is doing better every time he takes a practice run at the fort. He is definitely no FBI HRT (Hostage Rescue Team) Operator, but neither am I. Is he doing well enough that I think his odds of survival have increased if the shit were to hit the fan? Yes, as a matter of fact, he is.

Anyway, back to the Security office. We cleared the small 5 room building and in the last room, I found what I was hoping to find. Secured to the wall, with its doors standing wide open was a small arms locker. I counted a half dozen Beretta M-9's, 4 MP-5's, 4 M-4 Carbines, an M-14, a couple Remington 870 shotguns and my new baby, one beautiful M-16A2 with M-203 grenade launcher.

I actually received some training and experience with that particular weapon during my time in the Navy. I got competent enough with them that I was told by a Marine Staff Sergeant that if I ever tired of being a Corpsman, the Marines could always use a damn good grenadier.

Standing wide open on the other side of the room was the ammo locker. With the open pegs in the arms locker and the way some of the stacks of ammo were knocked over, I got the feeling that one of the remaining Coasties had grabbed some supplies and either took a last stand someplace or hit the road. Either way, I appreciate him, or her, leaving the doors open for us.

Once we got an idea of what was in the lockers we started moving everything up to the front by the door. There were tactical vests full of fully loaded magazines, cases of bulk ammo for all weapons, boxes of magazines for all weapons and four full cases of high explosive 40mm grenades. I get the feeling this was more of a load than this small station usually kept on hand, and they had received an extra supply of supplies when this whole thing started.

Derek was looking closely at one of the MP-5's so I grabbed a handful of magazines for it and stuck them in his pockets. Then I showed him how to insert one of the mags into the weapon and charge it. I instructed him briefly on how to best carry the weapon, how to use the sights, and how to fire it. He practiced bringing it in to his shoulder and up to a proper firing position before he commented that it felt very natural to him.

Since we obviously were not going to be carrying this stuff all the way back to the fort we needed to track down some wheels. By the front desk was a small locked cabinet which I hoped held keys. We popped the door open and sure enough, it was a key box. The top row said VEHICLES so we grabbed all of those keys and went outside. In the parking lot was a Ford F-250 and thanks to the way the government likes everything having a label on it, we matched a set of keys to the vehicle ID. I unlocked the door, hopped in, and tried the ignition, all the while hoping it would start for us.

I think someone was watching out for us because it did start, after several minutes of praying and cranking the motor. Just as she was about to completely lose the battery charge, she caught, choked to life and started to growl. We had a new vehicle with a full tank of gas.

We quickly loaded up the truck and I sent Derek back into the office to grab the last load of goods while I ran into the dispensary to grab my hidden cache of meds and whatever else I could find. No sense in not scavenging everything I could since we had a vehicle outside.

I had just dropped down into the waiting area from the pharmacy counter when I heard a burst of gunfire. I went running out of the clinic with my weapon at the ready to find Derek in a ready position scanning left and right with a zombie crumpled on the ground no more than 10 feet away from him.

I called out to him, asking "Slow mover, or fast?"

Derek replied that it was a slow mover and he had seen nothing else.

While I was commending him on the good shoot, he was actually cursing himself. He said the zombie was easily three times that distance when he first noticed it. He told me he was mad at himself because he took the time to put the ammo cans down instead of just dropping them. I told him that the fact that he recognized his mistake was a good sign, and that we would practice weapon transitions later.

For now we needed to hurry back to the fort. I was sure they heard that burst and were on pins and needles wondering what was happening. Combine that with the fact that gunfire always draws more zombies, and we did not want to waste any more time here at this location.

We got back to the fort just a few minutes later. Derek slid the sling of the MP-5 from around his neck and tried to give me it back to me, but I just told him to keep it, he had shown he could handle the weapon, and he earned it.

You should have seen the goofy assed smile on his face when I called him a Zombie Slayer.

We got the weapons handed out and had a quick familiarization session for those that had never experienced full auto. I have always been of the mindset that if you are going to have something in the house, everyone that lives there needs to know how to use it. I asked that everyone try to stick to the semi-auto operation after today though. There is no reason to burn through our ammo supply just because we have full auto.

I have seen too many movies where they dump an entire magazine in a situation where only one well placed shot was needed.

I did instruct them that if they are up against fast movers, switch to a burst and go for dead center mass. With the speeds they move, even a seasoned operator would have trouble making solid headshots. Let alone the clowns out there that claim they could make a 350 yard headshot on a zombie with an M-4. Not freaking likely!

Finding a cache of weapons like we did today has made everyone here at the fort feel good about things. It makes us feel like we could take on just about anything now.

This is also the kind of armament that would make me feel like we could take a Costco.

OCTOBER 16, 2009

Costco.

We have talked about it for the past couple of days, and after weighing all of the pros and cons, we have decided to go for it.

This is the one thing we have all said we would never do, and now we have a plan in motion to go in. Honestly, if this were a Costco in or near one of the bigger cities, we wouldn't be thinking about it, but with it being here on the coast, and us having been in the area with little to no activity around there for the past several months, it should be okay.

Two days ago we sent Harley over to scout it out. When he returned he reported that there is evidence that someone did secure the building from the inside, but he was unable to detect any noise or movement from inside the building. He told me he could smell some god awful smells from inside, but he could not tell if it was from the rotten provisions inside or if it was the undead. He counted approximately forty zombies on the perimeter of the building, all of them slow movers. That number would mean we would need to be on our toes, but still small enough of a horde that we would be able to take them out. I will be more concerned about the number of zombies we will attract once we start opening fire.

Harley said the road is relatively clear of vehicles with mostly organic clutter all over the place. This would be nothing more than branches and trash blown around by the coastal storms that go through here frequently. Ideally, we should be able to just drive right up to the Costco, get in, do what we need to do and get out, if that is what we are going to do.

There has been some talk about moving into Costco once we take it. However, we have also done a lot of work at the fort and have a decently established and producing garden. Nobody is wanting to abandon either location, so as of right now we are talking about splitting up the group.

Derek and Brenda are really wanting to move into Costco. As mentioned previously, Brenda has RA, and with winter fast approaching, we need to get her someplace that is dry, warmer, and a bit more comfortable than a replica of a two hundred year old fort. Since I still feel responsible for these two, I will likely be moving with Heather and them into Costco.

We obviously do not have storage capacity at the fort for the Costco haul, and it makes a lot of sense to just keep it here and have the two locations. This would also provide for a fallback location if something were to happen at either location.

As for everyone else at the fort, Wendy and John really don't want to leave their garden behind and they love the rustic living. Julie doesn't like leaving the area around the fort, and since Harley does not like being too far from Julie, he will be staying there as well.

That leaves Lars and Emily, who are definitely with child, to decide where they would like to be. While I think it would be best for her to be in the shelter of Costco, as well as being closer to me if something happens with the baby, they are leaning towards staying at the fort. I have to admit that with the supplies we should be able to get from Costco they can setup the fort, and make it even more comfortable than it already is.

Our plan to take the store is for Lars, Harley, Derek and I to take the building. Heather and Brenda will be driving the two trucks, leaving Wendy, John, Emily and Julie to watch the fort.

Our plan is to climb on top of the strip mall to the east of Costco and clear out the zombies from the elevated position. Once clear, we will drop down into the trucks and move to the main doors. Using bolt cutters on the chain Harley had told us was securing the front door we can then enter into the unknown.

That is the one part of the plan I really do not care for. I am not alone when I say that I would really like to at least have an idea of what is waiting for us behind those closed doors.

Harley has volunteered to go back with a plan to get on the roof somehow and cut a hole so he can see inside. I hate asking him to do it, but right now, he is the only one that can do what he is suggesting. We need to do that before we proceed any further.

OCTOBER 17, 2009

While the job is done, and Costco is ours, we are left wondering, was it worth the cost?

When we came back to the fort from the raid, John and Wendy met us at the gate with their weapons. They pulled Harley and I to the side and told us that Emily was gone.

They had been working with Fiona in the garden while Julie was sleeping under her bed as she usually does. None of them saw or heard anything. They looked all over the fort and were unable to find any sign of a struggle. There was no trace of blood, let alone anything else.

Harley looked over at Lars and told him his wife is missing. As you should be able to guess, he immediately lost it. He ran through the fort looking in every room, and yelling her name until he lost his voice. He wanted nothing more than to get out there into the surrounding area and search for her. Harley and I did everything we could do to console him and keep him from leaving, but Lars pulled his pistol and threatened to shoot us if we did not get out of his way. If not for Wendy and her staff, I'm not sure what would have happened. There was a whisper in the wind, a sound like a bat hitting a baseball, and Lars slumped to the ground.

For his own good we have him cuffed to his bunk for when he wakes up, and we have removed all firearms from within his reach. We left him armed with his blade and hatchet, but no firearms.

Harley left camp and searched the area for several hours, but he was unable to come up with anything more than a faint scent trail that stopped when he reached the waterway to the southeast.

This has been an extremely long day and we still have a lot of work to do. So while I want the rest of the day's events documented, I will make this brief.

Harley came back from Costco with the sunrise this morning with a report that the warehouse building was empty, nothing living or undead in residence. He could see a small cluster of corpses but could tell nothing more than the fact they were not moving. That information was good enough for me and the rest of the crew.

We quickly cleared the zombies from the perimeter of the building. At first I was slightly concerned as there were a lot more than forty zombies shambling around. Maybe the scouting activity over the past few days had brought them out of hiding. No worries. We did what we had to do and after about an hour of shooting, we had cleared them out of our way.

Once we were in the building we found exactly what Harley had told us we would find. Apparently, there had been a real live Jim Jones type event here. There were thirteen people of all ages and both sexes on the ground as if they had just lain down to sleep. Their cups were close at hand and the pitcher of the remaining poison was on a stool.

Harley and Lars dragged the bodies outside while the rest of us went to work doing a quick inventory up and down the aisles. By the time we got done with the dry food, the boys came to us with shopping carts for the meat. All of the meat and produce had spoiled long ago so we were just looking to get it out of there as quickly as possible. With a box of rubber gloves and a box of face masks from the pharmacy area, we loaded cart after cart with rotten meat and ran it out to the parking lot. It took us a few hours to get it all out there into a huge pile far enough away from the building that we felt safe enough to eventually set it on fire and let it burn.

The boys had already collected most of the bodies outside and had stacked them around the burn pile. Harley dumped a few gallons of kerosene around the perimeter, and Lars lit the match.

While they took care of the fire, I secured the front door with our own locks. There is no reason in leaving the place wide open for someone else.

As soon as we knew the fire was going to keep going we got in the trucks and split. None of us wanted to sit around and smell the stench any longer than we had to.

Then we came back to the fort to find this nightmare.

We have so many questions that need answers right now. There are so many emotions. Did she leave? Was she taken? If so, who or what took her? What's going to happen to Lars? In which way will he leave us, mentally, or physically?

I am a realist, I fully expect one of those two to take place, I know I would if it were me. Maybe we should just unlock him and let him go if that is what he chooses to do. We really have no right beyond our own selfishness to keep him from looking for her.

OCTOBER 28, 2009

It's been eleven days since I picked up this pen.

Eleven long damn days.

I wish I could take every single one of them back and try it again.

Lars is gone. He was gone when we woke up the next morning. Harley was on watch when he left and, well, nobody is really saying much of anything. Harley and I had removed his handcuffs while he was still unconscious. We also left his weapons and a pack with some rations by his bedside.

Maybe it is best that he left this way. On his own he may be able to find her. Then again, maybe he won't like what he finds if he finds her.

This is one of those Human Factors I have talked about so many times before.

Ultimately, it is best that he has gone to try and find her. I know this will sound horrible, but with him gone we will not have to worry about him going apeshit in the fort and doing something that will get me or one of the other people still here killed.

I am truly sorry that whatever it is that happened to her has happened. If there was a way I could change events, I would do so in a heartbeat, but I cannot do anything to change it. Since I cannot, I must do the next best thing that I CAN do, and that is to keep the rest of these people together, almost emotionally more than physically.

We have found that the best way to keep everyone together is by keeping ourselves busy. For the past several days that has meant Costco. We have been going back daily working on it, cleaning it up and getting it ready for us to move.

Derek and Brenda even started staying there the past couple of nights. We have created a living space in the middle of the store by taking apart some of the shelves to make walls around the area, leaving us just one way into the living area.

We were able to accomplish this by getting two of the forklifts running from the back of the warehouse. They run off of natural gas so as long as the tanks were still full, it was a relatively simple task. Once we had them running, we emptied a couple of the shelving units of their palleted goods. Most of it was wide-screen televisions that we will likely never be able to use anyway. We moved those around the doorways both inside and out, even using some of them to completely block off the side doors and any internal doorways to areas we will not need access to. You know, just in case someone comes knocking.

Then we used the power of the forklift to dismantle and move around these two shelving units. So, now we have a fortress within a fortress.

We also lined the floors with oriental rugs since we had stacks of them. We figured this would add an element of warmth. Couches and beds were moved into the area, some bookshelves, a dining table and one of their big stainless steel outdoor grills. With the amount of internal space, we are not too concerned about ventilation if we fire up the grill indoors. Add in an assortment of dishes, knives, silverware, cookware, glassware and we are all set.

Harley has turned over the radio he took from Julie's house and rigged several of the solar panels from the store up on the roof so we have some basic electricity. At least there is enough to keep the battery charged for the radio and run a couple of lights when we need them.

Fortunately much of the U.S. was working on becoming more and more green and self sustainable. The Costco chain was even slowly working on adding solar panels to most of their stores in order to make them completely self sufficient for power. Part of this movement was responsible for us being able to find the solar panels here that we did.

If this particular shit had hit the fan a few years ago there would not have been an ice cube's chance in hell of finding these consumer ready solar panels.

We have food, water, and miracle of miracles, the bathrooms are still working here. There is extremely low water pressure, but for now at least, we have flushable toilets.

We have also been working very hard to get rid of all the spoiled food in the place. Everything spoiled has been taken outside and burned, leaving us with nothing but dried and canned goods.

At this point in time, I would say that with just a couple more days worth of work, we should be at one-hundred percent.

It goes without saying that the one-hundred percent statement is only about the warehouse.

NOVEMBER 12, 2009

We have been moved into the warehouse and calling it home, at least for the four of us, for a couple of weeks now.

We have even begun to settle into a bit of a schedule.

We eat only one actual meal a day, typically in the middle of the day. Despite having a warehouse full of food we are making efforts not to gorge ourselves as we don't know how long we will be here or need this food. We tend to start our day with a protein shake, just to get us going.

Radio checks with the fort are done twice daily, once shortly after rising, and once before bedtime. Heather and Brenda take turns on the radio, monitoring all frequencies for, well, anything really.

It was just a couple days ago they caught some very faint radio chatter that Brenda was certain was Russian. From the strength of the signal compared to the capability of our equipment, they could have been a hundred miles offshore for all we know. Fortunately, they held off trying to communicate with the contact. I say fortunately because the only Russian boats I am aware of with that kind of communication capability are the infamous Russian Trawlers. High tech spy platforms disguised as fishing boats. We would like to stay out of the sights of the U.S. military, let alone the Russian military.

They heard something else yesterday shortly after waking up, but they couldn't make out what it was. It is possible that it was either

Morse code or "computer chatter". Neither one of the women was really able to tell us what it was they heard. They were doing a fairly quick scan of the frequencies before they realized they were hearing something and then they were unable to reacquire the signal.

Derek and I have taken to scavenging the Warrenton area for anything useful. We made it all the way to the City Hall our first trip out, and while we did find some zombies out in the streets, there were not enough to make it feel dangerous. This is the reason why we got out of the cities, lower populations! If a coastal town only had 5,000 people when at a healthy population, there would not be much of a zombie population to have to worry about.

We cleared City Hall of the few zombies that were inside then did a thorough search of the building. We eventually found what I hoped for: detailed maps of the town and the last census report detailing what families lived where and how many people in each family. It helps in a clearing operation to know if you should expect 2 zombies or 12 in a home.

On the way back to the warehouse that day we decided to hit the liquor store and grab what we could. Since all liquor sales in Oregon are controlled by the state, the one thing we did not have in the warehouse was liquor. Sure, we had plenty of wine, but sometimes you just want something a bit stronger. We cleared the building and set about loading a couple of boxes. I went back into the storage room and while there, I heard a scratching noise just outside the door.

I figured it was a zombie and since it is always better to fight them on my terms, not theirs, I decided to take it out. I opened the door with my weapon at the ready and saw... nothing.

There was nothing but a pygmy goat that had been grazing around the trash. This little guy was malnourished but still smelled like a distillery. He had obviously been eating from the trash here and from the way he was acting, I would be willing to say he was drunk.

I started to laugh when Derek came around the corner, saw the goat and said, "Can we keep him?!"

Now we have a pet goat living in the warehouse with us.

It's kind of bittersweet in a way as it reminds us of the pets we lost. Most of our pets had started dying off from the H1N1 virus. Once the first cat became infected and died from it, they started dropping like flies. Things got so bad with the pets that the government made the decision to start culling the animals, figuring it was best to control the spread in animals and hopefully prevent it from spreading to humans any faster than it already did.

In a way, Heather and I were lucky that our pets had died before the kill teams started coming door to door looking for pets.

I have to tell this story here as it has to provide some entertainment for someone out there, even if Derek would get pissed at me for spreading the word.

It was late in the evening, about 4 nights ago. Derek had said earlier he wanted to go for a walk around inside just to stretch. Brenda, Heather and I had been playing cards in our living space when we started hearing this noise from somewhere deep in the warehouse.

It sounded a little bit like music, so we grabbed our weapons and started searching the warehouse, trying to narrow down where the noise was coming from.

We finally found it, deep in the back corner of the warehouse. There in the corner was a big, comfy couch where Derek sat, clearly inebriated, with a half empty bottle of Jim Beam in his left hand and his right arm around the goat. The goat just sat there eating the remnants of a box of liqueur filled chocolates while Derek was beat boxing and talking to the goat.

Brenda started to laugh, and Heather and I started to crack up when Derek looked up at us and said, "I love this goat, man!"

So yeah, life in the warehouse is, well, it's a little bit like life.

DECEMBER 15, 2009

For the past few weeks now we have been working on a methodical clearing of the town of Warrenton, Oregon. Using the maps along with the census we took from the City Hall we started at the homes and businesses at the furthest distance from the warehouse. This way, depending on the time it takes us to clear and scavenge the town we have less distance to go every day. The basic idea is that the longer we are out here scavenging, the potentially weaker we may get. Get the more difficult work out of the way early on, and things should get easier as we go. In any case, an operation such as this you should always work your way from the outside in.

We have been bringing home truckloads of dried and canned goods every day along with bags of medication. Being on the Oregon coast, and surrounded by good hunting grounds we have also found a ton of weapons and ammunition. These have all been collected, taken back to the warehouse, and cataloged. Costco had started selling a couple of different sizes of gun safes back in the months before everything went to hell so we have been securing all firearms in those safes.

As of right now, we have six of the smaller safes filled to capacity, each one labeled with what is inside, Handguns, Long guns, Shotguns, Ammo, etc. Any ammo we have found for our everyday carry weapons has gone into our personal safes. We have also taken to grabbing whatever gold or precious stones we find. You never know when it might come in handy for something. Eventually someone, someplace will start the bartering system again and when it does, gold and jewels will be sought out.

And something else we have found is a bunch of zombies along with more than our fair share of corpses.

I now know what the rescuers in New Orleans felt after Hurricane Katrina, except ten-fold as far as the death. Not only that, but they were not having to kill what they found. Sure, they were fired upon a few times, but they were not having to deal with what we have been trudging through. Living on the Oregon coast where everything is cold and wet, a body decomposes fairly quickly. Trust me, there is nothing quite like going to lift a body off the floor and either pulling the limbs off or just peeling the skin off like taking off their shirt.

I have gotten to the point a few times where I question whether this is all worth it. To what end are doing this? Are we going to look for more survivors and attempt to repopulate this area? Put our backs to the sea and make one last valiant stand for humanity?

Shit man, I don't know, all I know is it is giving us something to do. We can either sit around and count days or we can get out there and do something that feels remotely worthwhile.

We enter a house, clear it of all zombies and dead, drag them out into the street and burn them while we scavenge the house. When we are done, we mark the house using the FEMA codes we learned a few years back, and then move on to the next house.

We have been doing between two and four houses per day. At around 1800 housing units and a population of just over 4,000 during the 2000 census, adjusting for those houses that no longer exist for one reason or another, we have a busy year ahead of us.

DECEMBER 18, 2009

Interesting happenings in the land of the dead.

Two significant things happened today, so the timing has to be more than just a coincidence.

Heather and Brenda were on the radio while Derek and I were out clearing the town. They heard the computer noise again, but this time they nailed down the frequency and wrote it down.

They then contacted Derek and I on our walkie talkies just as the drone went overheard. It was the same drone, black with crop sprayers flying about 150 feet overhead, that we had seen while out at the fort. This time it was coming from directly south of us and just as it passed overhead it banked slightly to the right and headed north-northeast.

I scrambled up the lattice on the side of the building we were working on clearing, and once on the roof I tried to watch it with my binoculars. With the dark paint job I pretty much lost it against the hillsides across the bay. I kept watching for several minutes longer, but was unable to reacquire it.

As I walked over to the edge of the roof to climb down the ladder Derek had put up for me I caught sight of the drone again. This time it was headed directly south over our heads. It must have reached a certain point headed north-northeast and then headed west, then dead south. I lost sight of it just as the girls called back over the radio saying they heard the noise again.

First the computer sounds over the radio, then the drone a few minutes later? Then the drone disappears just as the girls hear the noise again. No way in hell is that a coincidence.

With the apparent airspeed and flight time, it couldn't have flown much more than a few miles away, which would put it just the other side of the bay in an area we have not ventured into yet.

There are only a few things I can think of that are over there: a strip mall, an old motel and a high school.

After talking it over with Derek I think we need to take a trip to the other side of the bay. I have already contacted Harley and he will be meeting us at the warehouse early tomorrow morning.

DECEMBER 19, 2009

Okay, seriously, would anyone like to tell me just what the fuck is going on?

Derek and I picked up Harley and John at the crossroads and drove across the bay bridge.

Harley brought some of the gas masks we had taken from the Coast Guard Security office, so we put those on as soon as we came off the other side of the bridge. With that drone having the crop sprayer on it, none of us wanted to take any chances breathing whatever it had been spraying.

After a slow drive up the bay without seeing anything, we approached the high school on the left, and that was when we saw it.

There, covering the entire athletic field, someone had built a gigantic cage of some sort. Inside the cage were what appeared to be thousands of the fast movers, but they were acting strangely. Well, about as strange as something that was dead, but now has a heartbeat can act strange. They were mostly just milling about, and acting relatively calm. They were not freaking out when they saw us pull up, and trust me, they saw us.

I will never be able to forget the chill that ran down my spine when thousands of undead faces suddenly looked directly at us. It felt like nothing I had ever experienced, almost as if a thousand dead feet had just walked across my grave.

We had to dispatch a small handful of zombies that were hanging out around the outside of the cage. Even though we took them out with melee weapons, it did not take the zombies on the inside long to start surging against the walls of the cage. Fortunately, it looks like there is no way this thing can fail. Whoever built it, built it out of steel I-beams and two inch thick shielded cable. How the hell they built this thing without the entire city knowing about it is way beyond me.

Hell, with how they built, I want to know who built this thing? And who in the hell got all of these zombies locked up in there?

That was when it hit me, and I have to admit, that is one hit I would like to be able to give back. They did not put these zombies in here, at least not in the condition they are in now. They must have herded living, breathing people into this thing and locked them in. What could they have told these people to make them willingly enter a gigantic cage such as this?

As we got closer to the cage the zombies made no solid attempts to get excited or riled up in any way. They simply followed our every move like some undead school of fish. I have to admit, it freaked the fuck out of me when they did it.

Looking at them from as close as we dared get from the cage we could tell that they appeared to be not horribly damaged but they were all clearly zombie.

Even the noises they were making were different from anything any of us have experienced. They were nothing like the frantic screeching and howling of a zombie on the hunt. It was more like just a low throaty growl.

We did have a couple of them attempt to snap at us as we got too close to the walls, but they could not get through the holes no matter what they tried. It even seemed that, though they are still a bit "bitey", they almost appear to lose interest quicker.

Harley was starting to walk back towards the truck when he noticed that the walls had a coating of some sort on them. He reached out and ran his fingers along one of the cables, and what came off was almost like an ultra fine powder. Upon a closer examination, we saw that the same powder was on the zombies too.

Was this what the drones had in their crop sprayers? Were they really spraying some kind of a calming agent on these zombies?

We climbed back into the truck and got the hell out of there as quickly as we could. We need to figure out where this drone is coming from, and who the hell is in control of it.

All we know at this point in time is that the drone is coming from the south, and we have heard the same computer noise on the radio each time before it appeared and reappeared. It could mean that this thing is computer operated and is automatically doing this from some hidden location.

There are two things, however, that make me believe it is not being operated by a computer. Predator drones require refueling which means there has to be a ground crew. Also, we have seen the drone divert from its flight path. Computers tend to not make random variations in a flight path. A human, on the other hand, is more prone to randomness. That tells me that there are humans controlling this thing from someplace, and most likely from someplace close.

So, what we have is some son-of-a-bitch sitting in an underground bunker, flying this thing up and down the coast spraying zombies that are contained in an enclosure that could have only been built by the government with a powder that's making the zombies fairly docile.

Here is my question: why does it appear to only be making the hyper-zombies docile? It has apparently had no affect on the regular zombies we have encountered in the area, and since we dealt with that small handful of them outside of the cage, we know they have been sprayed as well.

Is there even the slightest possibility that they made them hyper-zombies to begin with??

Oh for Christ's sake, I need a drink and a tin foil hat.

DECEMBER 24, 2009

For the past 5 days Harley has been staying here at the warehouse with us, monitoring the radio day and night. Over the course of those 5 days we have heard that computer signal three times. Each time we heard it, we were able to run outside and see the drone going overhead just moments later.

Of course, this is now raising one very interesting question—why was it weeks between original sightings and now we are seeing this thing basically every other day?

We found a pallet of telescopes in the warehouse and have set up several of them on the roof aimed at the cage. From this elevation we actually have a fairly clear line of sight to the school and as long as there is no fog, we are able to see at least part of the cage.

This setup has allowed us to witness a spraying of the cage. The drone flew in, banked hard over the cage and started spraying. It took about 2 minutes for the spraying to complete, and then the drone straightened out, flew west, then took a dead south flight path and disappeared over the tree line.

It looks like our next step will be to head south and see if we can determine how far south it is flying. I keep thinking that Camp Rilea is south but that is a National Guard training base with no airstrip or hangers. However, at this point in time, it is our most likely suspect.

There is one other thing we have noticed that may explain the increased frequency of the drone appearances. On the mornings that the drones have appeared, the horde in the cage was getting more agitated. Even from our position a couple of miles away, with the telescopes we can see them acting significantly more aggressive.

When we were on location at the cage we did not see any cameras so we do not believe that anyone is actively watching the site. However, the predator obviously has a camera on board so whoever is flying it can see the state of the zombies. The resolution of the on-board camera is great enough they would even be able to see what their "mood" is before they got directly overhead, and would be able to make a spray/don't spray call.

As can be expected, the topic of conversation outside of the drone has been about the cage across the bay and the origin of the zombies. One theory that we have is that the government took every civilian that was left in Astoria, locked them up in the cage, turned loose a few zombies inside, then hit them with whatever it was that turned them into hyper-zombies. That is one hell of a conspiracy theory, but it would not explain why they are keeping them there and not exterminating them?

Another theory is that they realized it was the vaccinations, rounded up everyone that had received the shot and put them in the cage for their protection. Why would they have been so ready to go with the cage?

Yeah, it looked like it was pre-fabbed units and would have been able to be assembled quickly onsite. But why would they have something like this ready to go?

Unless, and this is just another theory, they had been working on a biological weapon and knew what was going to happen when they unleashed the vaccinations, only to have things get completely out of control. Jesus, I hope not.

On a sadder note, Goat took off today. We were sitting up on the roof watching the cage with the telescopes when I saw something out of the corner of my eye. Looking down, I saw Goat walking out in the road next to the warehouse. He gets out of a hole in the side of the building all the time so we just let him do his thing. About a half hour later I heard a zombie growl and looked down to see one chasing Goat down the street towards the highway. All I had on me was a pistol, so at that distance I would not have been able to get a good shot, and would have even risked hitting Goat. Derek had his MP-5 with him and after getting a couple of torso shots on the zombie he passed the weapon back to me. I hit him in the head on the second shot but the shot appeared to have scared Goat and he ran out into the highway. He kind of stopped and it almost seemed like he looked at us, but then he took off running south down Highway 101. By the time we were able to get down off of the roof, he was long gone. We went further south then we should have looking for a goat, but Derek did not want to give up looking for him. It was starting to get dark and there was some pretty heavy fog coming in off the ocean so we finally headed back to the warehouse. We'll miss the stinky little guy.

DECEMBER 25, 2009

Merry Christmas.

We saw that sucker land, it's Camp Rilea.

Harley and I hopped on some dirt bikes we took from a motorcycle dealership just down the road from the warehouse and headed south down 101. Since we had a suspicion it was Camp Rilea anyway, we headed that direction. We headed that way not really expecting to catch the drone before it took off, but with the notion of knowing where it should be when it returns.

We left Heather back at the warehouse with Julie and Fiona to watch over the radio. Wendy had sent Fiona in with Harley for a visit, and the kid wanted some face time with Heather. This left Derek and Brenda free to clear a couple houses while Harley and I were off doing our thing. They had a significant surprise waiting for us when we got back from our trip south, and that is definitely something I will discuss shortly.

Harley and I were headed south and sure enough, right on schedule, the drone went overhead, headed north.

A smile crossed his face as Harley gunned his bike and headed for the Camp. It was still bizarre for me to watch him ride the bike while missing his left hand. He had to reach over with his right hand and operate the clutch while trying to hold the bike steady with his stump.

We got there just a few minutes later and pulled up the main road to the camp. The gates were wide open and there were a couple of burnt out hummers, a few corpses, and a small handful of zombies, but no sign of any living persons.

We went ahead and blew through the gates, right past the zombies and then slowed down taking a drive around the main buildings. We had just turned right on one street when Harley saw the drone, off in the distance, headed straight for us with its landing gear down. It was coming in for a landing. Not only had we found the drone, but we were also directly in its path.

We drove forward to the south side of a small building that was just west of the road we were on. Even though it was a small building, it blocked us from any view by the cameras on the nose of the drone.

By the time we were off the bikes and getting our weapons ready, the drone had touched down and was taxiing down the street. We attempted to keep up with it, but I was holding us back. Even with all the weight I have lost, my knees still don't want to move like I wish they did in this cold, damp environment. Harley could have caught up with it easily, but he held back because of me. The best we could do was watch it turn right at what was almost the end of the road, then taxi right into the open side of a building. The door, basically the entire wall, came down just before we got to it. I thought about letting Harley take off after it, but it really doesn't matter now.

We know where you live you son-of-a-bitch.

When we got back to the warehouse Derek was sitting at the table with something rectangular and green in his hands while he was busy prying at it with a knife. Harley asked him what he had and his response was:

"Not sure, we found several cases of them in some militia dude's house. It says FRONT TOWARD ENEMY on it though!"

We screamed at him to please stop digging at it with his knife and to gently put it down on the table.

He looked up at me from his chair with a bewildered look on his face and asked, "Why?!"

"Because it's a claymore mine!"

Now, just so you know, Derek is six foot four, so he's a fairly big boy. That claymore went skittering one direction down the bench and he went flying the other direction, falling ass over teakettle backwards over everything in his way, all the while scrambling to dig his inhaler out of his hip pouch due to a spontaneous asthma attack.

Let me explain about a claymore mine, just in case you don't know anything about them. They are a 3.5 pound anti-personnel mine made up of 1 pound of C-4 plastic explosive covered with 700 1/8 inch steel balls inside of a convex shaped plastic box.

When detonated, due to the convex shape, it propels the balls outward in about a 60 degree fan-shaped arc, devastating just about everything in its path out to around 50 yards. In other words, it is a very effective killing device whether it is being used offensively or defensively.

It took several minutes for Derek's breathing to return to normal so we talked to Brenda about the mines. She said that while they did find several cases of them, they only brought back the one because they were not sure what they were.

She told us they also found several other large cases and big, heavy ammo cans that they were unable to carry out of the house. She also said that there were two big wooden crates that were too heavy to even move so they did not even bother to open them.

When I asked her if there were any markings on the crates she said that one of them said M-3 Tripod and the other one said M-2 HB. I looked at Harley at the exact same time he looked over at me. This is one of those things we loved about living in Oregon, it is what is known in the firearms circles as a Class Three state, meaning it is legal to own and shoot Class Three weapons. This gave us a higher chance of finding fully automatic weapons in our scavenging than we would if we were someplace like Southern California.

I know one thing, Harley and I cannot wait to see this house.

DECEMBER 26, 2009

I am starting to think that maybe God has not forsaken us after all.

Why do I say that? Because thank God for Oregon's large population of survivalists and its many militia members.

Derek and Brenda took us back to the house where they found the weapons cache. This place was a fortress. Made from cinder block, which I guarantee was cement filled and reinforced with rebar, it is a single story with 4 rooms, massive iron bars on the windows with a basement hidden beneath a heavy vault door in the back room. Try listing that with ReMax!

Covering the interior walls was this gawdy 1970's looking wood paneling and a ton of cheap artwork. I popped one of the sheets of paneling off the wall and was not too surprised to find several layers of kevlar lining the walls. This guy was either prepared for a fight that never came, or he was just plain paranoid.

With all of the conspiracy theory magazines and books we found in the front room, I half expected to find a hat-rack filled with tinfoil hats in the closet.

We never found the tinfoil hats, but we did find exactly what Derek and Brenda had said there would be. Yes sir, we found it, and then some.

What we took out of there was enough to start a small war in a third world country. Actually, I guess most of the world qualifies as third world these days, assuming this virus has spread around the globe.

Here is what we took out of there:

1 M-2 HB .50 cal machine gun with M-3 tripod

6 AK-47's, full auto, 20 magazines per gun

3 M-4 Carbines full case of 30 round magazines.

4 Mossberg 590 shotguns

6 crates holding 1 AT-4 rocket each

1 full pallet of ammunition for the M-2, 10,000 rounds

4 cases of M18A1 Claymore mines, about 50 total

20,000 rounds for the AKs and the same amount for the M-4s

10 cases of 500 rounds each of military buckshot

Christmas may have been yesterday, but we definitely got our gifts today.

I asked Harley if would take his bike across the bridge to the Ford dealership, and find us a heavy duty flatbed. The Ford F-250 I took from the Coast Guard is a good sized truck but it was not going to be big enough to get all this stuff back to the warehouse. By the time he got back with a truck we had the F-250 loaded with everything we could and were ready for Harley and his newfound strength to help get the big gun on the rig.

Harley asked me if I have any plans for this stuff as he had an idea he wanted to run by me. He started talking and it turns out we pretty much had the same idea.

DECEMBER 27, 2009

With the new arsenal secured in the warehouse we held a small celebration last night. Derek went out to the Fort to retrieve everyone and we proceeded to have a really good time. We drank, ate, talked and passed out way early in the morning.

This morning we talked about the plan Harley and I had touched on yesterday. While everyone is in agreement that it is risky, we also recognize the fact that there are easily a thousand or more hyper-zombies or more in a cage across the bay. If we are going to stay in this area, then we need to take the risk involved in getting rid of them. We either do that, or we need to consider moving again.

Now that we know where the drone is based out of, we consider it to be less of a threat. While it is something we should and will—look into, it is no longer something we feel the need to rush into.

For now, we need to consider the massive threat across the bay, and since we now have claymores and a .50 caliber heavy machine gun, the ability to do so has greatly increased.

As for our plan, this is what we have so far: Line the perimeter of the cage with claymores set to detonate in a daisy chain. Then we will have a second line of claymores outside of that ring. With the convex shape of the claymore, the explosive force would be focused inward, towards the middle of the cage. Upon detonation of the first line of claymores we would destroy a large portion of the zombies on the inside, but we would also damage the cables that make up the cage. If we wait approximately five seconds before detonating the second line of claymores, this should have allowed the zombies we eliminated enough time to fall to the ground, leaving us a clear firing line to take out another wave of zombies.

Since the first claymore detonation will likely severely damage the cables of the cage, the second series of detonations will surely finish them off. That will leave us with large gaping holes in the cage.

Considering that, if we mount the .50 on the back of the flatbed, have a gunner and an assistant gunner to help load it, we would still have room on the back of the truck for two more of us to provide small arms support. With three smaller weapons and the .50, we should be able to unleash a devastating wall of fire upon any zombies that are left over after the claymores.

We will also have a driver up front ready to get moving if they start getting too close. This should allow us to have just enough distance to be effective, but keep them off of us.

If we throw in some frag grenades and my M-16/M-203 for some low level artillery and I think we can do this.

Yeah, maybe, just maybe me and my guys can do this. Then again, maybe I'm a Mexican hat dancer named Pierre.

Here's the breakdown:

Derek will be on the .50, it will be secured to the flatbed and will not move. We will also lock down the tripod so he will only have side to side movement. He will also have his MP-5 for when he is being reloaded.

I know that having Derek on the .50 is a lot to ask. Number one, he has never fired the weapon. It is honestly not that difficult of a weapon to fire, but I wish we had the time for him to get some trigger time beforehand. More importantly is that he is going to be doing the most damage to the most zombies when we do this. This is going to take one hell of a toll on him mentally. But he is the worst shot of the bunch, so I need to place him on the trigger of the most stable weapon.

Harley will be his loader, and he will also be operating an M-4. While this may seem tricky with only his right hand, we practiced some reloads this afternoon and he will be just fine. As long as Derek is able to pull the bolt to the rear, we should be just fine.

I will be there with my M-16/M-203. That weapon will be significantly more effective if I am on the trigger. I spent a little time practicing reloading the grenade launcher while keeping the weapon up to my shoulder and in a proper firing position. I should be just fine.

Heather will be in the back with an AK. I'm not going to lie, I love my wife, and she is a damn good shot, I just wish I had someone else there instead of her.

John will be driving. He knows what is expected of him, and he knows what happens to us if he doesn't do it.

Harley and I will start on the ground beside the truck, each of us with a pair of AT-4 rockets. He will have the detonator for the first line of claymores, and I will have the second detonator.

As long as everything goes according to plan, the time-line should look like this:

Harley detonates the first line of claymores and readies his first AT-4.

I detonate the second line of claymores, ready my first AT-4 and Harley and I fire the four rockets into the crowd.

We jump onto the back of the flatbed with Harley beside Derek on the M-2, and me beside Heather.

Unleash hell on a legion of the walking dead.

End result? Well, we hopefully all get home in one piece and have a nice stiff drink and celebrate the victory.

We need to take a few days of rest to be ready and then we will do this.

DECEMBER 29, 2009

Harley contacted me on the radio the very first thing this morning and said he would be coming in for a visit, that he has something he wanted to show us before we headed out. I asked him what he had for us, but all he would say was that it was something we could really use when we go to take out the cage.

I would have never guessed what he had to show us, never in a million years.

When Harley pulled up with the truck I stepped out of the entryway of the warehouse and immediately fell to my knees in absolute disbelief. Over six months ago Lenny had walked out of the camp without a word, and now here he was standing in front of me with Gabe at his side. Lenny walked over to me and took me by the hand, pulling me up from my knees and directly to him, giving me the biggest bear hug I had ever received.

Of course I wanted some answers as to what had happened and how they both came to be here at this point in time. We went into the warehouse, took a seat and they started talking.

Gabe said he had left to reacquire himself and to try to find Lenny. He told us he had made it as far as the old encampment and found himself living there for the past several weeks. It was a week ago that Lenny and his family came hiking into the area.

Yeah, you read that right, Lenny had his family with him, Rebekah and all the kids were there. This would be the very same family that Lenny had told us he had to put down before he left Hillsboro.

Lenny was unable to look up from the table as he apologized for the lie. He had left his family bunkered down at his parents' place up in Washington. He told us the story he did so we would not go to get them until the bug out location was completely ready.

I told him he didn't need to lie to us, and that he should have said something when he left. He just shook his head and said, "I didn't want to impose on anybody, they are my family and they are my responsibility."

One of our own asking us to help him retrieve his family is no imposition. It would have been an honor to go with him.

I asked Gabe how he was doing, and in typical fashion he said he was solid, 100% with us and ready to do whatever we needed him to do, just after a little rest. I noticed his axe had significantly more notches in it than when he left. I kind of nodded my head in the direction of it and asked him how the hunting went. He reached over and ran his hand over the notches and said almost nonchalantly, "Business was good."

I took a few minutes and checked everyone out health wise while Brenda and Heather fixed them some food. Other than the expected blisters, cuts, scrapes and some slight malnutrition, they were all relatively healthy.

While they ate, we talked about the plan which they both agreed sounded plausible. At one point Lenny jumped up from the table and ran deep into the warehouse, coming back to the table with a bucket of laundry detergent. His thought was to dump out half the detergent, fill the bucket up with gas and mix it up. When we put the lid back on the bucket we would have a stable platform in order to place a claymore on top. Do all of that and we have one hell of a fugas bomb. A claymore combined with napalm? Sheer freaking devastation to anything on the receiving end.

Hell yeah! Why didn't I think of that?

Gabe will be taking the M-2 position on the truck since that was his weapon station in the military and he has the most experience with it. Lenny will be taking the position of assistant gunner and will now handle the reloading.

This allows me to have Harley step over and take Heather's position in the back of the truck and to be quite frank, I couldn't be happier. Like I said, she is capable, but she is my wife, and with that being said I would rather have her someplace safer than on the back of a flatbed truck shooting at a giant horde of zombies.

Derek will be moving into the position of driver, and John will stay home at the fort. He had no problems with this change in the plans as he is a bit of a pacifist and was not really looking forward to partaking in this wholesale slaughter.

With plans for the raid on the cage taken care of we sat down and had the somber discussion in regards to Lars and Emily. We talked about the circumstances of her disappearance and how Lars had taken off to find her. Lenny and Gabe both feel we did the right thing by not mounting a search party that night.

Having these two back with us where they belong has boosted my confidence in the success of this assault. They have asked for a day or two of rest before we do this, and we will give them as much rest as they need.

DECEMBER 30, 2009

Life in this post-apocalyptic world has handed us another day of sweet victory and vicious, agonizing defeat. Everyone we left behind at the fort is gone.

Wendy, John, Fiona and Julie are missing.

Gone, without a trace of blood, or signs of struggle, just like with Emily. None of the provisions or weapons were taken, just our friends, our family. One of the many things that pisses me off is the sickening taunt that someone had carved into the wood of the gate: CROATOAN

Just like the Lost Colony of Roanoke.

It would have taken several people to take all four of them. I know that John and Wendy would have done everything in their power to fight them off. I know they would have, because if I had been in their shoes defending my daughter, I would have died before I let anything happen to her.

Again, there is absolutely no sign of a struggle though. There are no empty brass casings scattered about, and no bullet holes. Nothing that would show that there was a firefight. We have been unable to even find any extra footprints that would give at least a clue that anything beyond day-to-day living had taken place.

I just don't understand this.

We have taken everything we could from the fort and have brought it back to the warehouse. We will return tomorrow or the next day to get the rest of the provisions. We have all agreed that it is time to keep everyone together.

In regards to the assault, it was an amazing fight and would have made for one hell of a video.

It took us a couple of hours to get all of the bombs in place, and this was getting the zombies inside the cage pretty well riled up. Quite a few of them were reaching through the cage walls and trying to grab us as we worked. We did a fairly good job of keeping our distance, but even then a couple of us wound up getting too close and were grabbed.

Yeah, I was one of them that screwed up. A female reached out and grabbed me by the collar, I pulled back and twisted myself around and just kind of stood there looking at her for a moment. I don't know what happened, I froze, that's all there is to it. Lenny walked by and with a quick slash of his machete he severed her arm at the elbow. Her hand fell from my collar and as soon as it hit the ground Lenny kicked it over against the cage. He smiled at me, I smiled back, and he pointed at the bombs and said, "We're ready."

Harley and I took our positions by the truck and he worked his detonator. The first detonations went off with only a couple of them being duds. A moment later I hit mine and they all went off, even detonating the bombs from the first line that had not blown. To be honest with you, we could have done it with a third less bombs. The fireballs were absolutely massive and if anyone were still in the area, they would have seen and heard it from miles away. The claymores cut a deadly swath into the cage and even through the flames I could see that a very large majority of the zombies in the cage perished in the blasts. No sooner had the second round of detonations gone off then Harley launched his first AT-4 into crowd. Another massive "whoomp!" and body parts flew everywhere. I fired my first rocket just as Gabe started hammering the horde with the fifty cal.

I launched a couple of grenades from my M-203 through the flames for good measure, and Gabe just kept sending bursts into the dwindling crowd. After a few minutes the big gun jammed and he was unable to clear it, so he picked up the AK from beside him and started firing. By that time we were pretty much left with nothing but basic clean up. Occasionally a stumbling, burning zombie would come through the walls of smoke and fire and we would take them down.

For the most part though, most of them perished before they even stepped out of the cage.

If this had been a military operation we would have been commended for our efficiency. We had killed hundreds, maybe thousands of the enemy in the matter of just a few short minutes. Thousands of what used to be human lives.

Combine that with what we found when we got back to the fort and none of us really felt like celebrating. Instead, we locked ourselves in the warehouse and drank ourselves to sleep.

JANUARY 1, 2010

Happy New Year! Seriously though, what is so happy about it? There was no crystal ball in Times Square last night, no celebrations around the world at the coming of the new year.

We have all lost so much over the past several months that this area has become so tainted for us that I frequently think of leaving and heading elsewhere. I do not even pretend to know where we would head most of the time, but anywhere has to be better than here.

I remember seeing an armored truck down in Seaside when Harley and I did the med run all those months ago. Maybe if I were to get my hands on it I could turn it into something some of us could live in and hit the road.

Who would I take with me? I know Heather, that's obvious. Derek and Brenda would want to go with us, so we might actually need something bigger than an armored truck. While I hate the idea of crappy gas mileage and supplies of good gas getting more sparse, I like the idea of having something heavy like that for pushing through what I am sure are debris-covered roads these days.

Lenny has his own family to worry about, and besides, they would need an armored school bus in order to accommodate them all.

Gabe wouldn't be able to deal with the confined space of it all. He needs more space than living in an armored truck could provide.

Harley is slipping away from us, little by little every day. Losing Emily and Lars, his best friends, in the way that he did. And then losing Julie as well. Man, I am keeping my eyes on him but I am not sure how much more the kid can take.

Even with these thoughts of abandoning our coastal retreat, we still have the desire to go after the drone and the people operating it.

I think that right now with all of our anger from losing another four people from our family, everybody that is left has itchy fingers and wants to get it over with.

I know I wouldn't mind some payback, and payback against anyone right now is what worries me. These are human beings we are talking about going after, most likely members of the military, and I have no problem with the idea of a firefight.

Is my grasp on reality slipping? Am I sliding precariously into the void of not caring about anything anymore? Quite frankly, it scares the shit out of me. Not only is it dangerous, but it is also how mistakes are made. Costly mistakes.

My friends need me to keep it together.

JANUARY 3, 2010

We have made the decision to go after the drone and the people that are in control of its operation. If nothing else, this operation will be for our own edification. We have to know who was responsible for the atrocity of the cage. Our only window of opportunity will be tomorrow since we hit the cage yesterday shortly after they sprayed it. I can only assume that once they do a flyover and see the destroyed cage that they will disappear. As of right now, the only plan we have is to head to Rilea first thing in the morning and wait until mid-day, when the drone usually shows up.

Since we will be doing an all out assault on what we assume to be a government installation, this will be a four man operation composed of just Lenny, Gabe, Harley and myself.

I am leaving Derek behind to protect the warehouse and the women and children. I have already given him specific instructions to head north if we do not return by tomorrow night. North, south, does it really matter anymore?

What does matter, at least to me, is that if we fail tomorrow, we can fully expect them to come to this location and destroy whatever or whoever is left.

Tonight? Tonight I will sleep for what may well be one last time with my wife and dream a little dream.

JANUARY 4, 2010

Not a single shot fired, that was how the day went.

We assaulted the base as soon as the wall opened up on the hangar. What did we find when we got inside? Let's just say we scared the crap out of a lab rat and an Air Force 1st Lieutenant.

Like I said, we entered the hangar as soon as the doors opened, sliding in past the predator as it headed out and down the makeshift runway. We searched the hangar until we found a slight trace of light coming from behind a tool locker in the back of the building. Lenny and I braced against it to push it out of the way when it swung away from the wall. Behind the locker was a small room, maybe 80 square feet or so, and in the floor in the middle of the room was what looked like a submarine hatch.

We opened the hatch and found a ladder down to a second level, approximately fifty feet down. Lenny went down first while we waited topside for him to give the all clear signal. Once he did we went down one at a time. At this level there was a long hallway with a series of doors on both sides. We did a quick scan and clear of each room as we passed it and found berthing areas, provisions, and a couple of server rooms. We finally found the operations part of the bunker behind the last door at the end of the hallway. As we stacked up and entered the room I almost thought we were going to give the two men in the room coronaries. The Lieutenant that was flying the drone completely lost track of what he was doing and flew the damn thing right into the bay.

At least the drone is now out of the picture.

The Lieutenant looked at his screens and calmly started flipping switches and pushing buttons, powering the system down.

Lenny was barking at him telling him to put his hands where we could see them and to his buddy on his knees by the table in the center of the room. Like I said earlier, we had an Air Force officer and a scientist of some sort. Those were the only two people remaining there. Apparently, they have had a pretty rough time as they started with over a hundred people at this location. With the amount of supplies and living space setup in the underground bunker, I believe them.

I asked the lab rat to give us a statement which I have reproduced here:

My name is Thomas Jenniches, I was the assistant to the head of the research department. With me here in bunker 59 is Lt. James McCartney, USAF, he is the Predator pilot for the program. This operation was joint USAF and Homeland Security. Our objective was to create an antidote for the vaccination victims that were referred to as zombies by popular media.

Yes, the vaccination was responsible for the current chain of events. The vaccination was fine, the problem was that between the time the vaccination was created and the start of the inoculations, the virus had mutated into something different. By the time anyone knew what was happening, death was followed by reanimation. It was too late, more than 10% of the population had been vaccinated in the first few days. It took us too long to figure things out and communicate to stop giving the vaccine. There were rural areas providing clinics weeks later, even doctors in larger cities were ignoring warnings from the CDC.

It was a royal clusterfuck.

We were sent here with a large military force to quarantine the city, evacuate all people not vaccinated and confine those that had been inoculated. That was why we had so many people in the cage. We needed them secure and someplace safe. They didn't all turn at the same time; some went quicker than the others. By the time we realized that was the case, it was too late. They started attacking the others in the cage. There were a lot of suicides after that. Many of the troops were unable to deal with the fact that they had sentenced these people to be slaughtered like that. I lost six of my cohorts that first night.

Work on the antidote was slow, tedious and dangerous. We kept losing people due to bites and suicide. Finally, one of the scientists from bunker 102 came up *with an antidote they said would work. They created the antidote in quantity and sent out dispatches to all locations. We were not the only ones working on this. Those of us here did not create the antidote; we simply used it, trusting the work of the others.*

As you now know, the antidote made them into something different. It returned some of the basic aspects of life but also gave them strength, speed, basic thought and advanced healing capabilities. What it did not do was remove the desire for human flesh. In trying to fix things, we made it worse.

We lost contact with the other bunkers within days. We set about creating an aerosol mix of a calming agent, number 399. I am not aware of its ingredients as I was not involved in that research. Before we were able to put it into wide use here at the bunker our research specimens broke loose and decimated everyone but James and myself.

Since that day we have done what we felt was our duty to keep bombarding the caged zombies with 399.

They denied any knowledge of us being in the area before today. They know nothing about the fort or our missing people and now that we have destroyed the cage and its residents, they feel relieved of their duty.

We offered to let them join us, but they declined the offer and based on the looks in their eyes I understood why. These men had simply done what they felt they needed to do over the past several weeks and months. Their feelings of guilt would never allow them to join up with the model of society we are creating. They were defeated and would take the final step as soon as we left the bunker. As they were clearly no longer a threat to us, we left them there with the means to do what they intended.

We thought that zombies were the biggest threat humans had ever seen. No, the threat is us, mankind. We tinkered and tweaked those things we had no business tweaking, all for the sake of humanity. By doing so, we not only failed humanity, but we have doomed it.

As we left the bunker, we heard two gunshots... and we never looked back.

JANUARY 13, 2010

With the double threat of the cage in Astoria and the drone being eliminated, we have settled into a routine of clearing Warrenton. With the addition of Gabe, Lenny, and Harley, we are now clearing more than a dozen housing units a day.

In his "free" time, Gabe has taken to burning out the boats in the harbor that have zombies on them. He had found a beautiful re-curve bow in one of the houses and immediately got a twinkle in his eye. He told me he has "always wanted to do this!" Basically, he stands in the parking lot and fires flaming arrows into the boats until they catch and burn. For now he only does one boat a day, making his entertainment last that much longer.

I have to say this though, I personally doubt very much that there are that many zombies left on that many boats. Seriously Gabe, we don't care, feel free to sink the boats. If you find it entertaining, go for it.

Heck, I needed a little fun yesterday and wound up pissing him off a little bit. Sorry, the high explosive 40mm grenades I use do a little more damage to an old wooden fishing boat than his arrows do.

Lenny has been working on a project for quite some time without having said much about it to any of us. He was clearing out a house that must have belonged to one of the many boat captains in the area when he found a bunch of nautical maps and charts. To say he has been extremely quiet ever since would be an understatement. These days he spends his nights with his family, his days clearing houses and the rest of his spare time with his charts.

Harley has been taking off as soon as we secure from our clearing operations for the day. I am quite certain he is out searching the area for any sign of our missing friends. I have to confess, I think it's for the best that he does this. It is giving him something right now that none of us are able to give him. Hope.

Derek has continued working with us clearing the houses. His back has been giving him some serious problems lately so we took a bobcat off a construction work site and he has learned how to operate that. He uses the front loader to shove the bodies into a central pile for burning instead of having multiple fires going in the street while we clear the rest of the houses on the street.

I know one thing; it sure has helped everyone to get that sickening smell away from us.

Brenda and Heather have even started helping to clear some of the houses out. I have identified those homes with only having one or two people living in them, and they have been clearing them out a couple of units per day. Not only does it help us get that much more work done, but it gives them something to do outside of the warehouse.

As for Lenny's wife, Rebekah? Well, she spends all of her time trying to keep their kids either entertained or learning. She has set up a little classroom in one area of the warehouse and is doing her best to keep them occupied. I went walking by the area the other day and Lenny was standing behind her with his arms wrapped completely around her and rubbing her tummy. Looks like there will be another one to add to the rosters before long.

It's been a long day so I took the liberty of dropping a couple of crab pots into the water down at the marina when we were finished with work. I went back down a couple of hours later and pulled them up and found a nice mix of dungeness and red rock crabs. We used to only be able to keep the male dungeness crab, but since we are the only ones pulling them out of the water these days, we tend to not pay too much attention to the sex. Crab is crab and even in the PAW we consider it to be a delicacy.

Brenda wasn't looking too well today, she said her rheumatoid arthritis was flaring and she felt like hell so she headed to bed early. She apologized for being a "party pooper" as she headed off to bed, but we all understand that this life is a long way from where she thought she would be two years ago. Hell, it is a long way off from where all of us figured we would be.

The rest of us sat around and drank a couple bottles of wine, talked about the future and the past. Things we miss, things we don't, people we do and definitely the shit we don't.

JANUARY 14, 2010
ENTRY BY GABE

I know Cole has been documenting everything that happens and maybe someday he will want to look back on this day, if for no other reason than in the hopes of finding the answers that surely must lie inside these pages.

Heather and Brenda are both dead. Brenda had apparently been bitten yesterday and turned either last night or this morning. We are assuming that she was bitten yesterday, but if that were the case, she turned faster from a bite than anyone that any of us have seen. I would have to say she had been bitten a couple of days ago, hid it from us, and the virus combined with everything that was wrong with her, and finished her off quickly.

I can appreciate that she was a good friend of Cole and Heather's but god damn it. Why did the bitch have to hide the fucking bite from us? A good woman is dead because of it and now Cole is off doing God only knows what.

Lenny has spent most of the morning trying to piece together the events as clearly as he can figure out. I have tried to assist him the best I can, just so we can give Cole some answers. As for Derek, he's a good guy and all that, but he's not my fucking responsibility. He may have taken off after Cole for all we know as none of us have seen him since everything went down this morning.

Upon examination we found that Brenda indeed had a bite mark on the upper back part of her right arm. It was freaking nasty looking and as black as death itself. There is no way for sure to tell when it happened to her.

Hindsight dictates that we should have been checking every one of us at the end of a day's clearing operations. We got lax and we failed to do what we should have been doing all along. We cannot allow freshman mistakes to kill us all.

From this point forward, anyone that is involved in direct contact with the zombies will immediately undergo a head to toe examination for bites as soon as said contact is complete.

With further investigation, it appears that Brenda was still alive when she woke up this morning. As far as we can tell, she went outside to throw up, and Heather was apparently helping her. They were just outside, and around the corner from the entrance. On the wall there were signs of fresh vomit and there were clean towels all around Heather's body.

Lenny figures that Brenda probably came to Heather for help, she may have taken her outside to keep from disturbing the rest of us. Brenda vomited, died, turned and attacked Heather. Heather had definitely fought back with her machete as she still had her right hand on the handle trying to pull it out of where it was stuck in Brenda's spine.

Heather had apparently tried to take her head off with the machete but hit at a bad angle, and stuck in a vertebrae. We give Heather this, the girl did not go down without a fight. Not only had she tried taking her head off, but she was also hitting Brenda in the head with a rock when Lenny finally showed up on the scene.

Lenny reports that he kicked Brenda in the side and sent her flying off of Heather. She started to get up with Heather's machete protruding from her neck, so Lenny fired one time, putting her down for good.

By this time we were all outside and looking at Lenny on his knees beside Heather. She was still barely alive as he held her hand. Cole dropped to his knees on the other side of her body and took her by the hand. Derek ran over to Brenda's side and dropped to his knees screaming in anguish.

It had been years since I cried as hard as I did when Heather looked over at Cole and said, "Thank you."

Through his own tears he asked her, "Why?"

Lenny let go of her hand and backed away, hiding his own tears as she told Cole, "Because I would have never made it as long as I did if not for you."

None of us could say or do anything as they sat there on the ground, savoring the last moments of her life. When she finally passed, Cole stood up, and walked towards Lenny, and that was when I saw his face and recognized the look.

Stopping beside Lenny, Cole said something to him, and then continued to walk away. Lenny turned around, walked back beside Heather's body and just as her eyes opened, he shot her in the head.

Nobody has seen Derek since he took off with a bottle of bourbon and his gun. If he goes to take anyone but himself out we will stop him, but then and only then will we do anything.

When you do read this Cole, know that we are here for you; willing and ready to do whatever needs done.

JANUARY 28, 2010
ENTRY BY GABE

It has been 2 weeks with no sign of, or word from Cole.
Come home soon brother.

FEBRUARY 2010

Heather and I always used to do the "what if" game in the BZ. You know, try to come up with answers to questions like:

What if the zombies rose and I got bitten, would you kill me then kill yourself or what would you do?

I guess now we know the answer to some of those questions.

Heather has been bitten, and she is gone. I asked Lenny if he would please do it for me, and as I walked away I heard the shot.

I thank God that I didn't have to do it. I look at that now. I used to have that bravado bullshit mindset that it would not be her, it would be a zombie and I would shoot her between the eyes without even thinking twice.

I now know why so many people died so quickly during the outbreak, they could not bring themselves to kill their loved ones, even those people that knew they needed to do it.

If not for Lenny I would have likely been another statistic, and even then I am left with the question of: Would that have been better than how I am living now?

I have been here at the bunker at Camp Rilea, hiding out for...shit I have lost track of time. I believe it is sometime in February but I could be wrong for all I know. I am certain that Lenny knows I am here as he has come to the bunker a few times and while I hid from him he would talk to me, telling me what is happening at the warehouse. I never responded and he never asked me to.

Many, many times over the past few weeks I have sat with a gun in my hand trying to find the weakness I needed to pull the trigger and leave this crazy ass merry-go-round we call life.

I say weakness because even now, in this fucked up world, I think it takes more strength to carry on and do what needs done than it does to pull the trigger, step off the chair, swallow the pills or cut the arteries.

Even in the BZ I abhorred suicides, viewing it as the coward's escape. Now the tables were turned and I wanted to be a coward for the first time in my life. I sought that escape, I desired it, I needed it.

However, every time I would bring that gun to my head, sticking it in my mouth, or placing it under my chin I would see Heather, sitting there, tears running down her cheeks. Every time she said the same thing, "This is not my Cole. This is not what he would do."

I have asked her what I should do because I don't know anymore. And every time she has given me the same answer, "Live!"

I think it was two days ago that I put my pistol in the holster and have not pulled it since.

I still talk to her and honestly, I am certain I always will. She was my soul mate and always will be.

She was right, I should live. I WILL LIVE.

MARCH 2010

I have forced myself to return to the warehouse as I feel that if I stay away any longer it is doubtful I will ever return. When I walked back into the warehouse this morning, I walked past Rebekah because I saw Derek walking around in the back and desperately wanted to talk to him.

Looking back on the day that we lost our wives I realize now just how badly I failed Derek as a friend. I had been selfish, I was not the only one that lost the love of my life that day. Derek lost his wife as well that day and I left him behind with relative strangers. People that, in spite of spending months with them, still treated them as if they were outsiders.

I called out to him to get his attention, and when he looked at me, he walked away, heading deeper into the warehouse. He did not stop to talk or anything, he just yelled out, "I am sorry."

I had to follow him around the warehouse for a half hour asking him what the hell he meant by apologizing to me. I finally cornered him and had to physically shove him into the corner before he said, "Brenda killed Heather, I'm sorry!!!"

I just grabbed this big man and hugged him tight and allowed the tears to flow from both of us. I told him I didn't blame him, I don't blame Brenda. We live surrounded by zombies, it was bound to happen sooner or later. We sat down and I told him about my thoughts while I was gone. We talked about the demons I fought and how close I came to taking the chickenshit way out. He admitted to me that he had come close to taking his own life as well. I asked him what it was that had stopped him?

He said he got a mental image of Brenda and I kicking his corpse and that had made him laugh. The absurdity of seeing his own corpse being abused by his loving wife and his friend was just enough to stave off suicide, at least for now. I can deal with that.

We talked for what felt like hours this morning before the topic of conversation finally came around to Lenny. I asked Derek if Lenny had talked to him and was told that he had been avoiding him. He said that Lenny has been clearing houses non-stop since the incident happened. He has only been coming back to the warehouse for five or six hours a night.

I was actually well aware of his schedule, along with the schedule of everyone else as I hid in the area and watched everyone for a couple of days before fully deciding to return. Not to mention the fact that I was pretty weak those couple of days, having not eaten much.

I was feeling much better since my talk with Derek and we both decided it was time to talk to Lenny.

We walked together into Warrenton. We even had to dispatch a couple of zombies as we went. Derek told me they have been seeing more zombies the past couple of weeks and they have grown accustomed to having to take out at least a couple of roaming zombies every day.

We finally found Lenny walking out of a small bungalow, carrying a decapitated zombie by the belt in his right hand. He had the fingers of his left hand tangled in the hair of the head, carrying it low at his side.

I called out his name and he dropped the dismembered pieces and turned to face us.

I told him we need to talk.

He said, "We'll talk later, now is not a good time!"

Derek and I both said, "No Lenny, we need to talk right now!"

Lenny started to shake a little, which was a little concerning to us, but he said, "About what?"

Derek and I walked up to him, extended our hands and told him thank you.

This proud warrior stood there and completely fell apart. We stood there, sobbing as he tried explaining to us how bad he felt that he had to do it, that he needed to do it, that he didn't want us to have to do it.

We kept trying to get him to understand that we in turn understood and that we are grateful he did that for us, while at the same time we expressed sorrow that he was the one to pull the trigger. I also reminded him that it was me that asked him to do it. He nodded his head and told me that while he appreciated that, he had already decided that day that he would not allow me to pull the trigger, he was going to do it for me.

If anyone had been watching this scene from a distance, it would have been one of near insanity: three large men, armed to the teeth, on our knees, hugging each other and crying almost uncontrollably.

Only Lenny suddenly drawing his pistol and shooting a zombie that was approaching us from our rear made it more of a crazy ass situation than it already was.

Tonight we ate and drank as friends, and I would like to think a little bit closer than we were before. If our wives are in fact watching over us, I am certain they approve.

MIDDLE OF APRIL 2010

We woke up this morning and started preparing to head out for the day's operations when Gabe stopped, looked around at all of us and then abruptly asked, "What the fuck are we doing?"

I started to respond but then it hit me what he was asking, and I have to agree, what the fuck are we doing? Why are we bothering with clearing this town? Do we really plan on staying here the rest of our lives?

That was when I asked the guys that very question, "Do we plan on staying here?"

Gabe looked over at Lenny and told him, "Go ahead and tell them brother. It's time they know."

Lenny spit a stream of Copenhagen across the warehouse floor, smiled and said, "As a matter of fact, I do have a plan."

Located in Astoria is a Coast Guard station, as we are well aware of by now. Permanently assigned to Astoria were three Cutters, the Alert, the Steadfast and the Cowslip. Cutters Alert and Steadfast were WMEC, or medium endurance cutters. 210 feet in length with a crew of 12 officers and 63 enlisted men. At cruising speed they have a 6,000+ nautical mile range. Cutter Cowslip was a 180 foot long buoy tender, typical compliment of 48 men and a range of 8,000+ nautical miles.

Lenny says that he and Gabe could most likely operate any one of these cutters, as long as they are still in Astoria. He also says that he has been working on charting a course to Alaska's inside passage where he says we could have our choice of islands where we could just stay and hunt, fish, farm, do whatever it takes to survive and finish out whatever time left we have on this planet.

We sat there and continued to talk about the details for hours. The more we talked about it, the more we got hyped about it. And the more we talked about it, the more we wanted to get the hell out of this place. Our biggest issue with bugging out of this location is all the work that we have done to clear this area. We are so close to being done with it that it would seem like a massive waste of time and effort.

However, would it be any more of a massive waste of time and effort to spend your entire life working for something, only to be so tired when it was done that you could not enjoy it? Yeah, so we spent a few months cleaning out a town and making it almost livable, but if life in the area sucks, what life do you really have?

I have to admit, I did think about the cage that is supposedly down in Seaside and realized that I don't have to kill every zombie I see. I don't owe anyone; I am not going to receive some grand prize for a zombie kill of the week or for having the highest head count. Fact is, I stopped counting coup a long time ago.

I think I am ready to just start surviving.

From the looks on the faces of the men surrounding me, they are too.

Lenny said that if the cutters are still there, they are probably full of fuel and fully stocked, ready to go. If not, we have more than enough provisions left here in the warehouse to get us to the inside passage and keep us going for months after we arrive.

We do need to decide whether we want to try taking the things to the ship, or bring the ship closer to us, then ferry it out on a small boat. Lenny and Gabe are both concerned that the water in the slough to the Warrenton marina would not be deep enough. The cutter has a 10 foot draught and they have not been able to determine the depth of the slough.

Not only that, but Gabe and I have sunk our share of boats in the marina. We may have a hard enough time maneuvering through it with a smaller boat to get provisions out to the cutter.

Since we may have a fight on our hands just getting in to Astoria to see if the ship is even there, I like the idea of bringing the ship closer to us and ferrying provisions to it.

As of right now, it looks like tomorrow Gabe and Lenny will go scout out the ship. If they are able to board it at that time and get it operating, they will attempt to bring it out and anchor it in the harbor. If they need more time, they will come back and we will all go the following day, that way we can provide cover or assistance in whatever way might be necessary.

I pulled Lenny to the side and asked him if he really thought they could operate the cutter. He tells me that every ship has what is basically an owner's manual of a sort that takes you through step by step on how to fire up the engines and get it underway.

Cool, I always wanted to take a cruise.

MID-APRIL 2010

As soon as Gabe and Lenny hit the road towards the cutter this morning, I hit the roof of the warehouse. If they were in fact going to be returning with the ship, I wanted to see it as soon as I could.

While I sat there waiting, I noticed that there really were significantly more zombies in the area. They looked like an extremely slow moving ant trail coming down off the bridge and headed into our general vicinity.

It's almost like a flock of birds migrating south for the winter. If not for the fact that we were a good five to six months away from our second winter here I might be considering that thought with more seriousness.

I called down to Harley and Derek and asked them to bring up some long range rifles and a bunch of ammo. The last thing we need is a bunch of zombies getting in our way when we start transferring provisions to the ship.

Harley grabbed a can of .308 ammo and pulled three hunting rifles out of one of the safes. Harley tied some rope to the ammo can and I pulled it up through the hole in the roof while Derek slung a couple of the rifles over his shoulder, and then followed Harley up the ladder.

From our vantage point we had a clear lane of fire out to the intersection. Harley said we should not shoot until they were in the intersection which gave us a perfect killing field. We loaded the rifles, flicked off the safeties and started firing.

We were shooting at a distance of about a hundred yards and I have to admit, I was pleased with what was happening. While it is not a long distance, and at least two of us could accurately shoot out to three or four times that distance easily, we were being quite the exhibition of efficiency. Three shots would fire, three zombies would drop. We were nailing head shots on moving targets at a hundred yards, consistently. You can't ask for much more than that. Typically, I would be the first one to say you should never shoot at a zombie at that distance, but with what we were attempting to do, the shoot was justified.

Meanwhile, the zombies were slow enough and sparse enough that quite often we had several minutes before another zombie or two would step into our kill zone. It almost became a game for us. We even started a rotation.

At one point in time I thought I heard some noise off in the distance but dismissed it as an echo from our shots.

After about an hour, I grew bored with the game and more anxious about what was happening with the guys and the cutter. I put my rifle down and started watching towards the city, hoping to see or hear something from them.

They had made the decision when they left to not take radios with them because of the weight. They wanted to travel as light as possible. I personally felt that was bullshit, a radio does not weigh that much, but they left without them. I really wished they had taken a radio.

It was about another half hour or so before I saw this large plume of black smoke rise up from the city. No fireball, no explosion, nothing of the sort. Just a giant puff of smoke.

Fifteen minutes later and I hear a ship's horn before I see it coming out into the bay. 210 feet of WMEC-623, the USCG Cutter Steadfast is ours.

The three of us on the roof went down the ladder into the warehouse where I asked Derek to watch over the warehouse and Lenny's family. Harley and I made our way to the marina and took the small tugboat that we had selected out to pick up the guys. They were standing out on the deck of the ship by the time we pulled up beside them. Gabe helped us tie off to the ship and we climbed aboard for a quick tour.

We quickly found that the ship was in fact full of provisions. Dry storage was absolutely full of food. There was actually enough food that from my calculations, they could have fed an entire ship's compliment for at least a month. Since there were only six adults and a small tribe of young children, we would have plenty of food for the trip North. With that being said, we will still want to take as much of the Costco provisions with us as we can.

Gabe said he will be staying with the ship. With it being at anchor there should be someone there to maneuver the ship if it slips from anchor. He said he will keep himself busy disposing of those things on board we will not need. He plans on throwing overboard chairs, tables, TV's, anything we will have absolutely no use for. That's fine as we will need the extra space for everything we need to bring with us.

Lenny did smile as he showed us something else below decks. The ship's weapons were on board. We had a small armory not to mention the two M-2 .50 cals and the M-38 25mm machine gun.

The M-38 mounting system was on deck and securely covered while the weapon itself was stored below. I have to say, God bless the Coast Guard, the weapons had all been properly stored with heavy amounts of grease. They should all be serviceable if we need them. Gabe said he will also take care of the M-2's and make sure they are in working condition. Even though we have the 2 M-2's on board, I still want to bring the other one on board. I refuse to leave an M-2 behind.

Starting tomorrow we will begin bringing the provisions over. First trip tomorrow we will also bring Lenny's family with us. He wants them on the ship as soon as possible. Fair enough. As we prepared to get back on board the tugboat, Lenny just started laughing.

I asked him what he was laughing at and he pointed at the tugboat, "Why didn't we just take the tugboat instead of risking our asses going through town?"

Hey, it was his plan, not mine.

APRIL 2010

We have been working on moving all of the provisions out to the cutter, and what an amazingly slow process this is. Much of the stuff we are taking with us is on palettes. So we are just picking them up, one at a time with the forklift, driving it down to the marina, dropping it off and returning for another one. While the forklift (me) is going for another palette, Lenny and Harley break down the palette and drag everything down to the tug. Typically, by the time I get back with another palette, they are ready for it. Since the tug is not huge, we have only been doing 4 palettes a day.

Gabe has steadily been working on the cutter itself, making sure it's weaponry is in shape and properly mounted, pitching all the stuff we won't need, and working on organizing the provisions as best he can. We are also going to be taking some furniture with us from the warehouse. They have a lot of stuff we could use if we are going to try to settle down on an island up north.

Harley has even talked about going over to the fort to see if it can be dismantled, placed on a barge and towed behind the ship. I guess he figures it would be easier to do that then it would be to cut down, shape and form the trees when we get there. Personally, I think the idea is way too farfetched, and way more work than any of us are actually willing to put into it. If you ask me, Harley is just wanting to put in a little more time searching the area around the fort. While I can appreciate that desire, I would prefer he be a little more up front with us.

Gabe tells us he was able to get the GPS on the cutter operating as most of the satellites are expectantly still in operation. We want to head north into the inside passage during the spring, so we need to get our butts in gear and start heading North as soon as possible.

Meanwhile, we are still seeing a trickle of zombies out of Astoria but at the rate they are moving they are truly nothing more than a nuisance. Just because it has been a while since I mentioned anything more about the zombies, please allow me to take this moment to write down a few words about them.

Their degree of decomposition seems to be advancing to the point where I don't think they can continue to be a major threat. The cold and the dampness of the northwest can rot anything, let alone the walking dead.

I have actually seen a couple of zombies that seem to stagger and then collapse into a heap on the ground. This goes back to what I wrote a year ago, no matter what, they are still a human body. Without blood feeding the tissue and even the bone (think marrow people!!) then things will begin to collapse.

I watched one that collapsed like a controlled demolition building. As it lay there unable to move I could tell that it was still "living", even though it could no longer move. This zombie could have been advanced in years before he ever become a zombie, I honestly couldn't say, he was that badly decomposed.

So to give a definitive answer on whether they will all come to this sudden end in time, or if this one was simply assisted in his decay by advanced age before he turned, I cannot give that answer.

Harley just came to me and said he is going to the fort tomorrow so I will close out for now. With being one man down we will have that much more work to do tomorrow.

APRIL 28, 2010

Harley called from the fort on his walkie talkie this morning, he was coming back from the fort, he was coming back fast and he had someone with him. He was pissed.

When he came flying into the parking lot of the warehouse he locked up the brakes on the truck, and came to a screeching halt before he jumped out of the cab and climbed onto the flatbed. He picked up a person wrapped in a tarp and threw him to the ground. As the body hit the ground the tarp unrolled, and inside was Truman.

We hadn't seen him in months. Now here he was, Harley had beaten him pretty badly but he was still climbing to his feet. I think I saw the reason why he had received the beat down he had. The very coat that Lars had been wearing when he disappeared was now hanging off the shoulders of the man before us.

Harley told us that when he got back to the fort early this morning he found Truman hiding under one of the beds. When he called out to him he slowly came out but was acting really funny. Once they got into the light Harley recognized the coat and started asking Truman questions.

He started lying immediately to Harley and then started to mentally break. He started laughing at him, talking to himself, crying, acting really crazy. Harley says he all of a sudden stopped doing those things, looked him right in the eyes and said, "They are all dead ! We ate them you know! We ate them all!"

I looked at Truman and asked him if this was true. Did he kill our friends?

He raised his eyes from the ground just enough to look at me as this sickening grin crossed over his face, "They were delicious, and we will eat you too. It is by God's will that we do what we do."

I don't remember even seeing Lenny move past me, but in a blur Truman was on his knees, holding his duct taped hands up to protect his face. I told Lenny to stop, I needed to talk to him.

Lenny took a step back and drew his pistol, holding it at low ready in case Truman started to make a break for it.

I stood there looking at him as intently as I could before I asked him, "Where are the rest of your people?"

Fucker just smiled at me and said, "I am God's vessel, exalted before all others, anointed by his blood and protected by Him. He will not allow you to hurt me."

I asked Harley if he would go into the warehouse and get my medical kit for me. It was just a moment later he stepped up beside me, handed the pack to me and asked, "What do you need me to do?"

"I don't need anything from any of you, this one is mine. Besides, he is the one that will be doing what I want done."

Truman asked me, "What will I be doing?"

I said, "First, you may put up a false front of bravery, then you might get a little pissed. Then, oh most definitely you will start to cry, and if you are as stupid of a son-of-a-bitch as I think you are, then the screaming will start. You might even pass out, but that's okay Truman, I can bring you back around and then we can start again. Once you think there is nothing else I can do to you to cause you pain, then I will really get started hurting you, and that? That is when you will start to talk."

This time, when I looked into those eyes... the eyes that I once mistook for belonging to a man that had nothing left to live for now held nothing but hatred and contempt. At least they looked that way until I shoved my thumb as deeply into the left eye socket as it could go. I dragged him screaming like that down the road to the nearest fish market, kicked the door open and threw him onto one of the stainless steel gutting tables. He started to try to get up from the table but Lenny shoved him down and helped me duct tape him to the table.

Lenny looked at me and said, "This is as far I can go with you Cole. You are about to go someplace I want nothing to do with."

I reached out for his hand, "Thanks brother, I'm already half-way there, I may as well go the rest of the way. I got this."

What I had to do to make him talk, I had to do in private.

Lenny said he would be on the building across the street, and would keep an eye on the building for me.

I stepped up beside Truman and asked him if he was willing to change his mind and would like to talk to me. He spit in my face and started reciting some kind of scripture. Now I have read the bible a couple of times, and spent a good many of my younger years in the church, but I never heard the scriptures he was spitting forth.

I cut off all of his clothing before starting with the basic finger torture. I stopped after breaking two of them as he barely skipped a beat in his scripture. When I cut off the pinky toe from his left foot he let out a slight cry, and the scripture stopped.

This was when he started preaching to me about his religion, telling me all about how the flesh of the innocent would cleanse his people and keep them safe from all attackers, undead and alive.

I bandaged his toe as I did not want him to potentially bleed out on me quite yet. While I finished taping it up I asked him again where his people were located, and his response was, "At the right side of God!"

For the next several hours I took little cuts with a scalpel at sensitive areas. When those did not work, I took deeper cuts. And when those failed, I cauterized those wounds with a blow torch.

None of it made him talk.

I finally thought I had something when I took an airplane bottle of 151 proof rum from my medical kit and poured it over his genitalia. He snapped his head in my direction as I lit a match, so I asked him again, "Where?"

More scriptures. I dropped the match into the alcohol and watched as the blue and red flame took hold. He screamed for a few minutes until I patted the fire out with his own shirt.

Okay, so the crazy bastard can take some pain. Time for the psychological torture. I tied a battle dressing around his head and started pouring water over it. Yeah, waterboarding. It worked against al Qaeda, I figured it would work here.

After about an hour of this Truman started sobbing like a small child, but continued to recite his scripture as soon as I removed the bandage from his face. Only this time it was different, he was telling me everything I wanted to know. In his bullshit he said there were "10 and 20 women and men at the end of the bay, North of where the dead people lay."

I asked him about the people he had taken, and if they were all dead. In his sing-song way he said he could not be sure, he said they had taken so many. I went through everyone and described them well enough to him that he was able to recall them all. When I mentioned Julie, he smiled slightly and said, "She is one of us."

I stumbled backwards upon hearing that, the rage inside of me threatened to explode if I did not hold it back.

I chose to not hold it back. I drew my blade and brought it down hard on the elbow of his right arm, completely severing it. I immediately dropped my blade and because I did not want this fucker dead yet, I applied a tourniquet to the stump and hit him with enough morphine to keep him out of it for the next several hours.

Now I just wanted to make sure the info he gave me was real.

Trust me, he doesn't want me to come back later after being lied to. When I told him this, I could see it in his one good eye that he believed me just before he passed out.

Julie, so she was one of theirs sent to spy on us, feel us out, get our numbers then get that info back to the cult. She had done this all in the name of kidnapping us, one by one. She used us all, especially Harley. God help them all when I tell this to Harley.

I stepped out of the fish market and called Lenny over to me. I told him a little of what Truman had said and Lenny confirmed that there was a small cemetery near the end of the bay as well as a cluster of houses that would easily fit the needs of a group of people that size. I asked him to hold onto that information until tomorrow morning.

LATE APRIL 2010

Looking back on the events of today, I should not have told Harley that there was a cult, or that it was anything more than one sick individual, or where they were. If I had done that, Harley might still be alive.

Instead, we will give him a wake fitting of a warrior.

After my talk with Lenny I secured the door of the fish market and did my best to sleep, but still keep my eyes on Truman. He did not move the entire night and barely opened his eye this morning when I gave him another dose of morphine. I leaned in to his ear and told him I would be back later for him, then walked out of the building. Lenny was standing there waiting for me and walked back to the warehouse with me.

When we got back I found the rest of the guys sitting around a table with a map of the area. They wanted to know where the bodies were.

I told them what Truman had told me, that there was a colony of 30 plus lightly armed men and women that were spending their time killing outsiders, sacrificing them in the name of God and consuming their flesh. Truman was apparently their leader and had told them that by doing so, God would protect them from the undead and make them stronger.

All of the guys were squirming in their seats from this information with emotions ranging from sadness to anger to disgust. I showed them the area on the map where Lenny and I believed their compound was located. Then I told them that Truman had admitted to killing Wendy and her family, and Lars and Emily. Harley asked me about Julie.

I hesitated too long to answer but when I looked into his eyes and told him that she was one of them, his eyes turned black. All emotion left his face, and I swear to God, I saw his soul leave his body. He turned and walked out the door. Minutes later, we heard his bike fire up and accelerate away.

If we were to do this, and take out these cannibal fucks, we needed to do it together, so we ran outside to try to catch up with him. He had cut all the tires on our vehicles. By the time we got our shit together and secured an appropriate vehicle he had a good 15 minute head start on us. Derek stayed behind to watch over Rebekah and the kids while Lenny and I chased down Harley.

I saw the smoke moments before I heard the gunshots. Harley was already there and from the looks and sounds of things he was inflicting massive damage. I can't blame the guy, they killed his best friend and his wife, and the woman he rescued turned out to be part of the people responsible for it.

We pulled into the compound through the trashed gates and immediately saw the bodies littering the area. Most of the buildings were already on fire, and Harley stood in the middle of the compound, his bloodied mjolinir hanging from where he had tied it tightly around his stump, while he methodically fired round after round from his M-4 despite taking hit after hit.

The kid had bullet holes in his arms, legs, his chest, his left ear was even blown completely off the side of his head, but he still fired his weapon.

Lenny and I did the best we could to locate and take out those defenders that were still firing at Harley. Just as we pulled the trigger on the last of the cannibals Harley dropped to his knees and screamed "Julie!"

I honestly expected her to already be dead, but she scared the shit out of me when she came running out of nowhere with a large hunting knife in her right hand, screaming bloody murder. Before we could get our weapons on her, she dove on Harley, driving the knife down into his chest.

I have to admit, what happened next I am still trying to process. I keep seeing it, running through my mind, trying to make sense out of it. Harley wrapped his arms around her, sprung up to his feet and ran into the main building that was completely engulfed in flames. You could hear her screaming for about 30 seconds before she was finally overtaken by the fire. We never heard a single noise out of Harley.

This had been the straw that broke the camel's back for him. I had seen him lose his parents in the beginning days, I took his hand at the wrist, he lost his best friends, and the girl he was falling in love with turned out to be a cannibal psycho that helped take his friends from him. I can understand why he did what he did. Enough was enough.

We came back to the warehouse this afternoon after throwing all of the bodies of the cultists into the fires. We needed to clean up the mess the best that we could. This was a scene we did not want witnessed by anyone else.

Anyone else?

Shit, there isn't anyone else out here. Not these days.

I walked back to the fish market as soon as we got back. Truman was still there on the table, but I could tell he had been trying to get himself loose. He looked at me with that lifeless eye and started begging for mercy. I took a handful of hair from the back side of his head with my right hand and grabbed his chin with my left. I pushed and pulled, turning his head around until the sickening sound of his neck breaking filled the room.

I did not stop twisting his head around until Lenny gently placed a hand on my shoulder and told me it was over. I let go of his head and looked down at my hands, they were covered in blood, and not just blood from the cleanup at the compound. My hands were covered in fresh blood from where the skin around his neck had torn. I nodded my head at Lenny and said, "Yeah, it's okay, he won't be eating anyone else."

MAY 2010

Nothing seems to make sense any more. I have started drinking way too much and I have stopped helping load the cutter. I even spent an hour today talking to Heather, trying to make some sense out of at least some of this.

Over a year ago, the world stopped being what it was. When it happened, we thought we would be this great group of people that would survive and start everything over. We had it all laid out, we knew what we were doing, how to handle the undead, how to survive, yadda, yadda.

I have lost my wife, my friends, my innocence and now I am thinking I have lost my sanity. I don't even know what day it is anymore, not that it really matters.

We have killed thousands upon thousands of zombies and we have now killed dozens of humans. What gives us the right to have made ourselves judge, jury and executioner?

What gave me the right to do the things I did to Truman? I practically tore his fucking head off just because I was so disgusted with what he had done.

Jesus Christ!!!

And people would have once thought I crossed the line by waterboarding him.

I RIPPED his head off! Who the hell does something like that?

I am clearly not the same man I once was. In many regards most of the changes I have gone through have been for the better. I am most certainly in better physical shape than I have been in many years but I have mentally slipped deeper into the darkest chasm I have ever been in and I am not sure I can climb back out of it.

Yesterday I realized it has become as easy for me to destroy a human life as it is to destroy a zombie. That is clearly not normal, and to be frank, it scares me.

I am beginning to question if I should even be around people any more.

Maybe I should go before I become the Human Factor for these good people.

MID-JUNE 2010
AN OPEN LETTER
FROM YOUR FRIENDS

Cole,

You have been gone now for six weeks with no word, no sign and by now we are not expecting you to ever return. I have been back to the Rilea bunker just in case you had gone back there, but have found no sign of you to date.

In the event you do return, we wanted you to have these words so you would know that you were missed.

We have all read your journal and have collectively come to this conclusion, you are far from a monster and no more insane than the rest of us.

We have all been by the fish house and discussed what happened there that day. Yes, the things you did to him would be looked upon as atrocities in any civilized society; there is no doubt about that. However, this is far from being a civilized society anymore.

What you did, you did for us, and they were a result of the insane acts his cult perpetrated upon our people. Honestly, not one of us would have done anything differently. Perhaps not as cleanly or methodically as you did, but we would have done our best.

If the actions you have done failed to bother you, that would give us cause for concern. Instead we have watched it tear at you and bring you to the brink of total collapse. We understand why you left, while at the same time we wish you would return.

Yes, your humor is dark and your temper is quick, but your compassion for us is as deep as your loyalty.

Steadfast is loaded and ready to go. Also, we have been tracking the satellites for the weather systems and we feel strongly that we should head north at any time.

Know that if we are gone by the time you return, we waited for you as long as our window of opportunity allowed. I do not want to go, but I have to put the safety of my family first and need to get them North.

If you do not return in time but would like to join us, we are heading for an island at the bottom of what would be considered part of Alaska's inside passage. There is an inlet that we should be able to take the Cutter into that may offer enough cover to hide us if someone does happen to go past the island. You know what to do with these numbers: 54.928256, -133.015280

We wish you Godspeed.

Your friends,
The Kings of the Dead

MID-AUGUST 2010

This is my first journal entry in what I believe to be months. For the past several days I have been recuperating here in the warehouse, slowly regaining my strength and health.

I had left for a while to find…well, what exactly did I expect to find? An answer? A guru on a mountain top? Myself? Yes, maybe a little bit of each one of those things, but I also left because I knew that in the frame of mind I was in before I left, I was a danger to my friends.

What I wound up finding while I was gone was a notion. A notion that if I am anything, then I am nothing more than a product of my environment. Since my environment is a fucked up, upside down world, then I am simply doing what I need to do in order to fit into that world.

I feel that I am no more insane than the next guy. No matter how hard I tried to convince myself that I had gone insane, the simple fact of the matter was that I am not.

Sure, I stood outside the rusting cage of hyperzombies down in Seaside and thought about finding a way inside to join the hundred or so that were in there, but would that be insanity or fatigue?

Yeah, okay, so I occasionally talk to my dead wife. Does that really make me insane, or am I just some poor bastard finding a way to cope? If it makes me insane, then good, I don't want to be anything else.

Which of these two examples is a crazier notion?

Example A: A man who talks to his dead wife, lives in a world where the dead are out to eat you, and is willing to do whatever he needs to do to survive.

Example B: A man who works fifty hours a week for fifty years only to die of exhaustion a few years after retiring.

Personally, I am now ready to be the man in example A. I worked for twenty plus years for the military, the federal government, multi-billion dollar corporations, and slinging food in restaurants. Looking back, knowing what I know now?

I wish this shit had started years ago.

So, I am back at the warehouse, and unfortunately I returned from my journey just a few weeks too late. I had walked up to the bridge first to look at the cutter but it was gone. I used the last of my energy to run to the warehouse and found my journal, open to the last entry, sitting on a table at the entry way. I quickly read the letter and realized they had left. I knew that what Lenny had said at the bottom of the note was true, there would be a time that his family would need to take priority. That was completely understandable and I would feel like hell if I expected anything but that to be the case.

I guess I asked a question out loud, "How long ago?"

I am not really sure about what happened to me, but the response from the darkness of "Twenty two days!" was the last thing I remember. I can only guess that I must have passed out from the shock and malnutrition.

The first thing I remember after waking was to look up and see Derek sitting in a chair, watching me. It did not take him long before he started telling me everything that had taken place while I was gone.

To me, the most important thing was that he had made the decision to wait for me to come back. He took a huge personal risk on me ever returning. Even he says he is not sure what he would have done if I had not returned, or how long he would have waited.

He did say that in his gut he knew I would return eventually, and that when I did, I would need a friend. Since I was there for him at the beginning, he felt he should be here for me at what may well be the end.

We have talked non-stop for the past couple of days about what we will do. He has asked me if I want to go north to join up with the others. I would like to get up there, but I feel there are a couple of other things I have left to do beforehand.

I do know one thing, we can't stay here any longer... I am quite certain we have stayed well past our welcome.

SEPTEMBER 2010

Derek and I have been in the process of gathering our supplies, making inventory of what we have left and deciding what is essential and what is not. We have plenty of weapons and ammo, food, water, clothing and bedding, now all we need is something to carry it all in.

I still like the idea of the armored car from down in Seaside. Sure, there is plenty of room for us to sleep in and nobody is going to get inside unless we want them but, they have to be crap on gas mileage. So we would have to figure out a way to carry as much gas with us as we possibly can.

While I like the idea of a tank, I also like the idea of having something lighter and more maneuverable, so I got my hands on a couple of BMW R 1200' motorcycles and have been teaching Derek how to ride. He has actually learned the basics fairly quick so now all we need is a trailer and the armored car from Seaside.

Since all we have done is ride around the parking lot here at the warehouse I wanted to take Derek on an actual road. Riding around a clean parking lot is nothing compared to a road covered with debris of all sorts. We rode out to the cultist's compound because Derek had not been there and really wanted to pay his respects to Harley.

We got out there and the place was nothing but a total burn out. Since the fire had been allowed to burn uncontrolled, there was nothing left. All of the buildings were gone with nothing but piles of charcoal and ash sitting on the foundations.

I kind of gave Derek the play by play of what happened that day, and told him about how Harley had jumped into the fire with Julie hanging on his body.

Derek was acting stunned, walking around in a bit of a daze looking at the remains of the buildings when he called me over to what was left of the main building. Where Harley had jumped into the fire there were signs of only one body having burnt there. I climbed down into the foundation and dug around in the ashes with my knife. I found first one, then two hands, it wasn't Harley.

That leaves me with one question, where the hell is his body?

SEPTEMBER 2010

We took the bikes down 101 and headed into Seaside. There was minimal contact with zombies on the way with just a few on the sides of the road on the way into town, and just a handful of zombies once we were there.

I told Derek about the hyper-zombie cage on the southern end of town, and how there were only about a hundred or so in the cage. It was much smaller than the one back up in Astoria, but this group of zombies also acted differently. They were calmer, and did not get as excitable as those up North. Considering the hyper-zombie cage and what happened when Harley and I came down here the first time, I made sure Derek and I were on high alert status.

The armored truck I had seen so many months ago was still there. My biggest concern was that it had not run in well over a year, would we even be able to get it started?

The tires were still inflated, the doors still opened and fortunately for us, part of the driver was still in the driver's seat with the keys in the ignition. I tried turning the key, it started to turn but quickly ground to a halt. No luck. I had brought a pair of jumper cables and hoped that the motorcycle would be able to give us enough juice to at least get it started.

It almost killed the bike so I had Derek hit the gas a little more and with absolute luck, she choked to life. We opened up the rear doors because we were going to need to put at least one of the bikes in the back. There were more sacks of money in the back of that truck than I had ever seen in BZ life. There were sacks that had the names of all major banks on them even some that said Federal Reserve.

It didn't take me too long to figure out that whoever had been driving this truck in the final days was intent on keeping this money. Now, it is nothing more than paper that is only useable as a heat source, insulation, or compost. It truly is not worth a thing.

We shoveled most of it out of the back of the rig and using a bench from the side of the building we muscled the one bike into the back. Derek drove the truck while I followed on the other bike and we hit the road. When we got close to the warehouse, I passed Derek and got to the building first so I could open the bay door so Derek could just drive it right inside.

We spent the rest of the day working on it, cleaning out the rest of the money that was left, and stacked it to the side. The shelves on the sides came out quite easily and within a couple of hours, we had an empty shell. It is definitely wide enough for two cots, one on each side, provisions on the floor and walls and plenty of weapons and ammo for the both of us.

At one point in time I turned to Derek and said "Man, I wish we still had one of those fifty cals!"

He just smiled at me and motioned for me to follow him back into the warehouse.

Back in a corner under a tarp, was the fifty we had pulled out of the survivalist's house so many months before. Derek told me he had talked the guys into letting it stay with him in case I did return.

Awesome! Now if I can just figure out a way to mount this thing in the truck.

SEPTEMBER 6, 2010

$1.1 million dollars. That's how much money was left in the truck after we shoveled out the first few bags of it. That is a lot of cheddar, but it is cheddar that does not mean shit in this world. Anyway, we did more important things today than just count paper.

Today we mounted a pair of plow blades to the front of the truck and not just because it looks cool. With placing them at the angle we did it will help us push through a horde of zombies with significantly more ease that if we just had a flat front end.

While at the motorcycle shop I also picked up a pair of roof top cargo containers. We can mount those to the top and fill them with extra provisions. It never hurts to have a little more than you already have.

Since the U-Haul shop was right next door to the motorcycle shop we were also able to grab a trailer and hook it to the flatbed.

I even had to kill a couple of the zombified U-haul guys that were locked in a supply room. That's just kind of par for the course these days though. While it is getting rarer and rarer that we see a zombie, few days pass without having to kill something in this world.

I grabbed a couple of spare trailer hitch balls just in case there wasn't anything on the truck. Of course, once I got back to the truck it already had a hitch on it so that was a waste of time. I went ahead and tossed them into the truck any way just in case.

I was looking at some of the stuff in the back of the shop and I might be able to use some of their tools to work on a project I have cooking in the back of my mind. Maybe later, once we are closer to being ready to hit the road, I will wrap up that project.

Derek had grabbed some tarps and stuff and was loading them on to the flatbed when I came out. I bent down to pick up one of the pieces that dropped and as I did, Derek fired a shot, hitting a zombie right between the eyes. Damn thing had stepped out from between the buildings and I had never seen it.

Back at the warehouse I mounted the plow blades while he worked on his project in the back of the truck. After a few hours he called me back into the rear to show me what he had done. Using the tarps and some metal poles taken from a chain link display in the back of the warehouse, along with some of the chain link fence material, he had made us our cots. He had even taken a couple of the twin sized memory foam mattresses from the warehouse and trimmed them down into pads for the cots. I have to be honest with you, they are pretty damned comfortable.

Now we have plow blades on the front, a trailer for the bikes and beds.

In the next few days I am going to see if I can mount a couple of solar panels from the roof on the top of the truck. It would be nice to have at least enough electricity to be able to keep the batteries for our flashlights charged up. Not looking to power a plasma TV or anything, just a little trickle charge. I am also going to look into the possibility of some kind of external racks for the sides of the truck. I only need them to be big enough to hold a few five gallon gas cans. While fuel is the one thing that we have a reserve of right now, we have no idea what our fuel situation will be when we leave the area.

Speaking of that, we have not taken the time to talk about where we will go when we leave here. I don't really want to head south. Warmer weather and larger population centers are not exactly something that I want to head into. If we head north we will be staying in the same environment and that is a big part of what I am wanting to get away from. Obviously we will not head west as we are already as far west as we can go.

It looks like we will be heading east. That was easy.

SEPTEMBER 11, 2010

I got the .50 mounted in the back of the truck today, and even I have to admit, this is too freaking cool.

What I wound up doing was building a flexible arm that folds flat against the ceiling of the truck and locks into place with a set of safety pins. When the arm is down, the gun is securely mounted to a platform that allows for side-to-side as well as some degree of up and down movement. I had to cannibalize the tripod to help build the actual mounting platform but my initial tests have proven it to be strong enough. Building the entire mount out of steel rectangular tube helped in the strength department. I almost think this mount is strong enough to handle a pair of 50's.

The only problem with my setup is, this weapon is an M-2 HB... a Heavy Barrel. Overall length of the weapon is 65 inches, with a barrel length of 45 inches.

We were not able to close the doors with the arm fully extended as the end of the barrel stuck out the back door by almost two feet. It took me longer to cut the barrel down than it did to build the damn arm. But I guarantee that I now have the only 24inch barreled .50 cal mounted in the back of an armored truck. Sure, accuracy is now blown to shit but that is not what I am looking for here. While the standard fifty was accurate out to a few thousand yards, I only need something to chew through a horde of flesh eating zombies.

No, this big sucker is my version of an OSP. An OSP stands for Oh Shit Pistol and was what I used to carry in my pocket more often than not back in the BZ.

I held a concealed weapons permit for many, many years. I had to take a bunch of classes and pass local and federal background checks just so I could carry a gun. I was the good guy. The people that did not understand guns always thought I was scary because I carried a gun. They never stopped once to think that I was the safest person to be around. On top of the classes I had to take, I took additional classes. I always wanted to make sure that if I was ever involved in a shoot, it was going to be a "good" shoot, and with greater chances of walking away unharmed.

Anyway, I am drifting off-topic, something I have been doing a lot of lately. Derek has told me more than once lately to shut up, that I am drifting. There I go and do it again.

Okay, an OSP. Mine was a little .38 special snub nosed revolver and the reason it is called an Oh Shit Pistol is because if you ever have to pull it out, that is most likely what you are saying, "Oh shit!!"

That is what this M-2 has become... a weapon that will not be that accurate at a distance, but devastating to anyone or anything that is close enough. Not only that, but it looks cool.

Derek keeps telling me he is going to paint eyes and a mouth on it.

I keep telling him, "Don't paint the fifty!!"

I am thinking I might have to kick his ass.

We finished loading the truck and trailer this evening and decided to not waste any time. We leave in the morning.

MID-SEPTEMBER 2010

He painted the .50.

Dammit! It actually looks good. He painted it like the P-40's flown by the Flying Tigers in World War II. Snarling rows of sharp teeth with eyes on either side of the receiver. Okay, it works.

We have filled all of the gas cans we can get our hands on and have filled the racks on the sides of the truck with 8 cans each side, 2 cans on each rear door, with another 12 cans in the trailer. That's 22 cans of fuel at 5 gallons a can. This truck has a forty gallon tank to begin with so that gives a total load of 150 gallons, at probably 10 miles per gallon, that's a decent stretch of road covered.

We started to hit the road this morning, and as we pulled out onto 101 I looked in the rear view mirror for one last look. As I did, I caught something moving just as I looked away. I hit the brakes and sat there for a moment watching what appeared to be a zombie standing in the middle of the road, just looking at us.

I told Derek to stay with the truck, I needed to check something behind us. I got out of the truck and slowly walked back down the road with my pistol drawn. The zombie was there in the middle of the intersection and started to act like some kind of trapped animal. It was looking all directions, as if it was not sure which direction to go.

It turned to run back towards the trees when I called out to him, "Harley!"

He stopped at the side of the road and turned to look at me as he dropped to a crouch, ready to flee in an instant.

My god, the kid looked like a burn victim, his face was not recognizable and his body was covered with remnants of his clothing fused to his skin. I could even see the hilt of the blade Julie had driven into him still protruding from his chest. I can only assume that he had jumped into the fire with Julie and then self preservation took over and he ran out the back of the burning building.

I said his name again, "Harley?"

Through his burnt and retracted lips he hissed, "No Harley. Just pain."

I asked him, "What can I do to help Harley? I will do anything you need me to do."

He spastically shook his head, then looked me directly in the eyes and stated as much as he asked, "Kill me!"

I told him "No, I can't do that Harley. Please don't ask me to do that. Come on man, you will heal, we have seen it before."

He looked at me and slowly shook his head. I could tell every word out of him took immense effort and caused him great pain. "No heal. Pain."

I tried to offer him pain medications, alcohol, anything that might ease his pain, but his only responses were that he was in pain and that he wanted to end it all. Finally, realizing there would be nothing I could do for him, I offered him my pistol. He held up his right hand, and showed me that his fingers had been completely burnt off his hand that day. Even if he could hold the pistol in his hand he would never be able to pull the trigger.

I pulled the gun back and stood there looking at it for a moment. When I looked up at him he was begging me to do it. I then asked him, "Forgive me?"

He nodded his head gently, then lowered his head down so his chin was resting on his chest. Knowing I would likely talk myself out of it if I hesitated at all, I raised my pistol and pulled the trigger. Immediately I turned around and started walking back to the truck when Derek jumped out yelling out to me, "What the hell was that?"

Closing the distance between us as quickly as I could, I climbed into the driver's seat and told him, "Just another zombie."

He stood there for a moment looking back down the road, and I could tell he almost headed back there several times. I finally told him to just get in the fucking truck.

We drove in silence through Astoria and headed east on Highway 30. We took it nice and slow today, more out of necessity than anything, there were a lot of cars on the road, accidents, abandoned trucks, overturned semis, it looked like a real war zone out here.

The closer we got to Portland, the more cluttered the roads became.

We were seeing more and more corpses and military vehicles the closer we got. We even came across a pair M-1 Abrams tanks that scared the shit out of me until I realized they were dead where they sat.

I went ahead and stopped and had Derek cover me while I scavenged what I could out of them. I was able to grab another two partial cans of .50 cal API (Armor Piercing Incendiary) ammunition, a spare barrel for our M-2 and an M-4 carbine and a bandoleer of ammunition that was still in one of them. The M-4 had some surface rust on it but after a quick visual inspection I dumped five rounds down the barrel and it worked just fine. I also grabbed two cases of MRE's that were tied to the back of the lead tank.

Not a bad haul for a little stop and shop.

I don't really want to go into Portland so if we can stay on the outskirts I will be happy. At the same time, I would like to see what has happened to the city in the almost two years we have been away. I just hope the main bridges over the river are still open and we don't have to go too far out of our way to hook up with I-84.

We have decided to sleep on Sauvie's Island for the night, doubting that there will be many zombies on the other end of the bridge. We pulled up over the bridge and found a barricade. Jumping out of the truck to see if we could move it we were taken surprise by someone calling out to us. There were survivors on the island.

Their story is that most of the farmers and full time residents had been able to hold Sauvie's Island while the rest of the area fell. They have subsisted off of what they grow on the island combined with all of the livestock. Considering the fact that the island is almost the same size and shape of Manhattan Island, but with almost one hundred percent of it being fertile soil, they should be able to last a good long while.

Once they had determined that we were of no more harm to them than they were to us they opened the barricade and allowed us onto the island to spend the night. We ate a wonderful dinner with them at one of the leaders' homes and shared our story of survival so far in return. After drinking more hard cider than I should have had we were offered beds for the night, which we gladly accepted.

I have to admit, it was nice to see a group of survivors that were actually doing better than us.

SEPTEMBER 2010

We headed out early this morning after the farmers offered to top off our fuel tanks along with a couple more 5 gallon cans. When offered additional fuel, you need to go ahead and take it.

We got back on to Highway 30 and went east. The closer we got to Portland, the slower it went. We were already only traveling about 30 mph and had to slow down to 10 to 15 mph just to maneuver around all the cars and trash on the roads.

There were multi-car pileups, scenes of frantic firefights and cars full of zombies still stuck in their seat belts.

We finally got to the northbound 405 bridge and found it to be absolutely packed full of cars. Southbound was still packed but not as bad as the other direction. Things really looked like most people had been heading north. We got on to southbound 405 and as soon as we got to the I-5 interchange we were blocked again. There was no way we were going to make it going this way.

Derek and I both uttered "Shit!" at about the same time as we realized we were going to have to go through downtown.

We got off the highway and got onto Burnside Road thinking it would be the widest road available and sat there for a few minutes talking about it. Do we haul ass and try to blow our way through or just take it nice and easy?

We chose nice and easy figuring we would wind up with less damage to the vehicles that way. Besides, the last thing I want to do on day two of this journey is to kill our wheels. It wound up taking us more than two hours just to get across the Burnside Bridge from I-405. Even on high traffic days in the BZ, this is a trip that would have only taken about 20 minutes.

Although, I have to admit, there were far less zombies in downtown Portland than we were expecting. Now, with that being said, when we went over the bridge we saw that Waterfront Park was jammed full of them. Even with more of them down there than we came across on the main roads, we ran down an awful lot of them as we went.

We even got to share a laugh because we ran over zombie Elvis. See, you have to understand Portland has always prided itself in being different. Bumper stickers everywhere proudly proclaim "Keep Portland Weird!" Well, in the BZ in Portland we had a street performer that dressed up in a nasty old Elvis jumpsuit and attempted to sing like Elvis. Problem was, he never washed his clothes, looked nothing like the King, let alone sing anything like him. Honestly, it was a pleasure running him down.

I just laughed and looked at Derek and said, "Yep, Keep Portland Weird brother!"

We finally got on to I-84 going east, and stopped at the truck stops in Troutdale. They looked relatively clean from the highway so we went down for some supplies. Sure enough, the parking lots and tanks were clear of any walkers. Unfortunately, the shops themselves were filled with zombies. With all the doors chained shut from the inside there was no way were going to get anything from inside.

Locked from the inside and full of zombies? Somebody had let the wrong ones in.

I took a moment to tighten all the nuts and bolts for the plows just in case they had either vibrated or jarred loose during the drive through town. Considering all of the zombies we had plowed over or pushed to the side they were holding together quite well. Derek took care of the fuel situation but was unable to pump any fuel from the tanks so we loaded back into the truck and hit the road again.

We drove past The Dalles and took the Highway 97 bridge across the river into Maryhill, Washington. I took us to the Maryhill Museum of Art figuring it would be a good place to crash for the night. Since I did not think too many people would have been out looking for art in the final days, we did not expect to find too many zombies in the area.

The building was still intact, and luckily for us the front doors were unlocked. Once we entered the building we gave the immediate area a quick once over just to make sure nothing would be right there to surprise us. After we were convinced there was no horde hiding out inside we chained the doors and we were secure for the night. Honestly, this place was built to last with its steel I-beam and poured concrete construction combined with the heavy doors and bars on all the windows.

Deeper into the museum we eventually came across a couple of zombies. One of them looked like he might have been overnight caretaker or security officer, it was kind of hard to tell. I shoved him into a broom closet and barricaded the door.

Derek asked me, "Why didn't you just kill him dude?"

"Why bother? I'll let him out when we leave tomorrow. No sense in keeping him from his duties."

I'm pretty sure Derek said something along the lines of "Fucker is getting crazier every day." I can't really bring myself to hold it against the guy as I know without a doubt I am barely hanging on right now.

SEPTEMBER 2010

When I opened the door to the broom closet this morning, the old man was standing there looking into the corner. Propping the door open with a can of polishing oil I left him there to find his way out into the museum and eventually resume his duties.

Heading east , we eventually got to Pendleton and took the business loop off the main highway just so we could see how bad it looked. The town was empty with only minor problems on the roads and minimal zombies. While Pendleton was a small town by most standards, with an original population of close to 20,000, we needed to be on our toes as long as we were here. Down at the other end of town was a sporting goods store, so we decided to go on a shopping trip.

Like I just said, the town was relatively clear and the doors on the store were wide open. As in they were tied to the bumper of a truck that was sitting across the roadway with its doors wide open. We walked into the store as cautiously as possible and found that the place had been ransacked. There were only a few rifles that were left on the racks, and absolutely no handguns or shotguns left. We were able to find a couple cases of Mountain House dehydrated food on a high shelf in the storeroom. We took those out to the truck and I told Derek I wanted to go back in, and for him to keep an eye on the truck.

I went back in because I wanted to check the offices. When I found them the door was locked with a handwritten sign on the door saying "Alive Inside". I knocked on the doors and got no response so I went back out to the truck and grabbed my shotgun with the breaching rounds. The door opened with one shot, allowing me to enter the office. The unmistakable smell of death immediately hit my senses as the door pushed open. Sitting in a chair in the middle of the room was the badly decomposed corpse of an older man, no visible entry wound but one hell of an exit wound in the rear. Crumpled on the floor around him were the remains of a pair of women. From the hair I would have to say one of them was significantly older than the other. It is possible that this was a family, but that is something I will never know. I picked up the pistol that was on the floor beside the man in the chair and opened the cylinder. It was a five shot .44 Special revolver and three of the five rounds had been fired.

Murder/suicide. What a bitch!

I dropped the pistol to the floor and took another look around the room. There was an aluminum firearms case on the desk with its lid open. A couple of 1911 pistols and few magazines loaded with good defense ammo were in the top section of the case. I closed the lid and flipped the case over and opened the bottom section. Nothing but a handful of crappy little pocket knives that were worthless to me. I pulled them out and left them on the desk. Walking out of the office I never even bothered to look back.

We decided to stop for the night here in Boise so I pulled off the highway at the Cracker Barrel and that is where we stayed for the night. Cracker Barrels would be at almost every highway off ramp from here to the east coast so this will give us a good idea of what to expect for supplies as we go. The front doors were secured and all of the windows were still intact so we walked around the building. I found a corpse half in and half out of the back door. Giving it a boot in the head I made sure it was really dead before dragging it outside. Derek and I cleared the restaurant without finding any undead so we made sure everything was secured and settled into scavenging everything we could.

You know those Jack Daniels Cakes they used to sell in the Country Market side of the restaurant? Oh yeah, they are absolutely FILLED with preservatives. Hopefully, by the time I am done eating, I will be able to wake up in the morning.

SEPTEMBER 24, 2010

We are sitting outside of Cheyenne, Wyoming for the night. To say it has been a long and interesting few days would be the understatement of the decade.

We made it through Idaho easily enough, and were even able to refill with fuel in Juniper just before passing into Utah. We had spotted a gas station quite a way off the highway, but it looked like there were not a lot of cars around the building. We had learned that the more cars, the less chance we had of finding any fuel. We drove out to the station and as we pulled up I saw an old man sitting on a bench with a shotgun across his lap. Derek and I looked at each other a little flabbergasted, but I cautiously opened my door and stepped out of the cab of the truck.

The old timer stepped around the corner and said, "What can I do for ya?"

I was still dumbfounded, but I told him we needed some diesel if he had some. He walked over to the pump, fiddled with the nozzle and started to fill our truck with fuel.

I asked him, "You do know what's going on out there, don't you?"

He looked at me oddly and asked, "Now what are you talking about son?"

"Well, the riots in the cities, the dead walking the earth. Honestly, there are not very many of us living people left."

He spit in the dirt by the pump and scratched his head a moment, "That sure might explain a few things I reckon."

I asked him, "Things like what?"

"Like why my wife tried to bite me, and why I ain't had many customers in a while. I figured it was the damn truck stop down the way taking all my customers."

"So, you did not know about this stuff? Don't you watch TV?"

"Ain't got much need for one, no radio either."

The trigger on the fuel nozzle released and he triggered it a couple more times just to make sure we were topped off, then he looked at the pump and said, "That'll be sixty-two dollars even."

Derek reached behind my seat and pulled a handful of twenties out of the bag of money we had kept and passed them my direction. I counted out four bills and told him to keep the change. He took the money, thanked us and walked back to his bench and sat down.

I looked up at Derek, who was sitting there with the biggest 'what the fuck?' look on his face I had seen in quite awhile. Shaking my head I climbed into the truck and we headed back down to the highway. Laughing about that crazy old man kept us going for quite awhile.

Going through Ogden, Utah, was another story altogether. As we got into the outskirts of town, we found barricades across the highway, with signs plastered all over the place reading "STAY OUT." The thing that bothered me the most is that while there were several emplacements for guards, there was nobody manning the stations. It almost seems as if somebody had tried holding the city together but failed.

We passed through the barricade at the outskirts of town and headed up the remarkably clear road, driving deeper into the downtown area. There were plenty of wrecked cars on the sides of the road along with signs of firefights and mass burnings all over the place. No matter how hot your fire gets, there are still going to be traces left of what you have burnt. There were enough identifiable remains in the ash piles to know that someone had been burning an awful lot of people on this stretch of highway.

We were about 5 miles in when I caught a flash of something in my rear view mirror. I looked back and was able to make out a pair of vehicles. They looked like Chenoweth off-road vehicles... and they were coming on fast. They pulled up beside us, one on either side of our vehicle. There were two people in the one on my side and only one on Derek's. They were all dressed in what could have been military uniforms, or they could have just dressed up like they were military.

They motioned for us to stop, and Derek asked me not to but I told him we would be safe as long as we stayed in the vehicle. I pulled to a slow stop, but kept the engine running. Derek and I both slid the barrels of our weapons out the firing ports built into our doors. The passenger on my side of the vehicle stepped out and raised his hands in the air.

He identified himself as Ranger Hanson, of the Ogden Rangers, as if we were supposed to know who they are. Apparently, around fifty National Guard troops stationed in Ogden had been able to band together and stop the tide just before the city was completely wiped out. The Guard members had taken on the name of the Ogden Rangers and had taken on the responsibility of saving Ogden and as many of the cities citizens as they could. They only had a few thousand people in a secure area, but it was a start.

He kept his hands above his shoulders and neither one of his drivers ever took their hands off the wheel. Since I did not see any signs of aggression or deception, I lowered my guard and got out to talk to him face to face. He told me that while the Rangers have kept peace and order in the north, a rather nasty group of raiders had claimed the southern part of town. They had been watching us since we got within 5 miles of town, and did not want us going into the area blind. I guess there are some people out there that still care about getting another person's blood on their hands.

I thanked him for the information, and wished him the best of luck with his town and his Rangers. I also commended him and his troops for their dedication. It was nice seeing someone else that has been able to hold on.

I asked Derek to drive and I grabbed my M-16/M-203 with some extra ammo and climbed onto the top of the truck in between our two storage units. Before we took off I asked Derek to take it nice and easy with me up there. While I was in a fairly safe place, I was still on top of a moving vehicle. With him driving at about 20 miles per hour, I was actually left with a very stable platform in case we did have a run in with some raiders.

I could see the final barricade off in the distance when a truck came flying onto the highway from a hidden on-ramp. As the old Bronco flew up beside us I got a good look at them from under the storage unit to my left. This bunch of assholes had seen Road Warrior one too many times. I kid you not, they had everything down almost perfectly.

Derek was doing everything as we had discussed, he was keeping his speed steady and in a straight line. Even when the idiots swerved in on him he kept the vehicle steady. That helped me as I stood up and pointed my weapon down into the passenger compartment. The passenger was standing in his seat so when he looked up he was less than ten feet from the open maw of my grenade launcher. He dropped into his seat with a scream and the driver of the Bronco slammed on his brakes and did a power slide, winding up facing the other direction. I thought for a moment about launching one into their ass as they took off like crazy headed the other direction.

We made it to their final barricade without further incident. About five miles past the barricade I signaled for Derek to stop so I could get back in the truck. He pulled over and we both took a moment to stretch our legs.

We were grabbing some water and using our gas cans to top off the tank when we saw a zombie slowly walking up the road towards us. She was blonde and except for a pink tank top and bloody panties, she had nothing else on.

Derek just kind of chuckled and said, "Looks like a witch, dude!"

I looked at her for a moment and for whatever reason, I felt pity on her and wanted to put her down. I raised my gun to fire. Just as I squeezed the trigger, Derek hit the underside of my arms with his hands and yelled "Don't! She's alive!"

He was right, she was not a zombie. This was a young girl, maybe 15 or 16, with massive scars around her wrists and ankles, showing signs of having been tied up for many months, maybe even years. She came walking right up to me and through split lips and broken teeth said, "Help me," as she collapsed into my arms.

While she was unconscious, we stripped off her clothes and did the best we could to clean her up with what we had available to us. We needed to check her fully for any signs of bites or infection. We figured since she was already unconscious we could do it real quick and without any problems.

All I can say is this: she is free of bites and infection. But, the signs of massive physical and sexual abuse were too much to not notice. This poor girl has been through the worst kind of living hell imaginable.

We got her dressed into some of our spare clothes and laid her into one of the beds in the back of the truck. I told Derek to hit the road and head east; I had some work to do in the back.

I got an IV going in to her. She needed fluids and needed them fast. I also gave her a catheter so I could get some fluids into her bladder, really hoping for no signs of kidney failure.

She is malnourished, dehydrated, anemic and beaten. I fed a vial of Rocephin, a broad spectrum anti-biotic, into her IV bag hoping it would not kill her from an allergy standpoint but also in hopes that it would stop any possible infections she might have.

That was around two days ago. She is still unconscious, and I am actually to the point where I wonder if it is worth using any more of our supplies to help her. She might be too far gone both physically and mentally for me to do anything about either one, and all I am doing is delaying the inevitable. I don't like the idea of putting her out of her misery but I really don't like the idea of just putting her on the side of the road and driving away.

We need to figure out what we are going to do.

Meanwhile, here we sit at the Little America Truck Stop just outside of Cheyenne, Wyoming. We have been able to refill our fuel and have even found a good supply of dried goods inside the store.

Derek has spent most of the time opening and searching trailers looking for anything useful. What he has found has mostly been truckloads of electronics and other goods that are worthless to anybody these days. However, he did find one smaller truck that was filled with beef jerky and other well preserved junk food. His response? "It's better than tofu!"

We might need to stay here another day or two just to rest up and figure out what to do with the girl.

SEPTEMBER-OCTOBER 2010

Her name is Kimmi, with an "I" not a "Y". She is 17 years old and states she has been on her own since the day the zombies pulled her mom out of their mini-van on the way home from soccer practice. That was almost 18 months ago.

Obviously, she woke up this morning, the morning I was going to regretfully do what I needed to do. Isn't it funny how things work?

I was sitting there on the right side bunk trying to find the strength and courage to pick her up and take her out the back of the truck when all of a sudden she opened her eyes and said "Kimmi".

I am not going to lie, I broke down into tears. All this time I have been taking lives, both alive and undead, and I finally got to save one. We immediately got her some of the Pedialyte I had taken from the warehouse and made her take little sips, just a little at a time. Even then she threw some of it up.

When she got enough strength together she told us about her mom dying and how she ran from the van all the way home, only to find nobody there. She said she stayed there for several weeks hoping someone in her family would come back. Nobody ever did, at least nobody she wanted to come back.

She told us of the night they came for her, four or five men, how they broke into her home that night, how she tried to run, how they caught her, how she tried to fight and what they have done to her since they have had her in their custody.

She has been pregnant twice, losing the first one within weeks, and going full term the second time. Immediately after the delivery the baby was taken from her, and none of us want to know what happened to the baby.

She has told us about her family, a younger sister, her parents and her extended family and her friends. She has also asked us what we were going to do with her. When she told me she would "earn her keep" in order to stay for us I was quite taken back. She said that sex means nothing to her now, and if we will take care of her, she will "take care" of us.

Derek and I have both assured her that neither one of us want anything of the sort from her. We simply want her to know we will both do everything in our power to keep anything from ever happening to her again.

She was so tired she continually fell asleep throughout the conversation. Without a doubt, this has been the most she has spoken in months, if not years, and it has used every bit of energy reserve she has built up.

Right now I am thinking we will stay here at Little America for a few more days, at least until she gets enough energy back to be able to hit the road.

MID-OCTOBER 2010

It is somewhere around the middle of October, and I either have a birthday in a few days or it has already happened. Not that it or any other date really matters anymore.

Kimmi has finally gotten to the point of being able to walk around without getting tired and has been able to run at a sprint for close to a couple of city blocks. I told her I needed to know she could make a run for it if we needed to once we were back on the road. She jumped out of the back of the truck, ran across the parking lot and back to me without being too winded. She is good to go, so we finally hit the road this morning.

As much of a show as she put up with her run across the parking lot, it took a bit out of her to do so. Kimmi is now resting in the back of the truck but has not stopped talking about the trip ahead. She told us that her family had never traveled beyond Ogden very much so she was excited about what she would finally be able to see.

You know, I was too, especially after almost two weeks at that truck stop, I was getting the itch to go.

We drove about 100 miles east of Cheyenne today and we are currently sitting in the parking lot of the Cabela's main store in Sidney, Nebraska. I expected it to be completely emptied of anything scavenge worthy and for the most part it was.

I was able to get some more size appropriate clothing for Kimmi, along with some good shoes. So at least now she will not be swimming in our clothes and when she needs to run, she will be able to do so in significantly more comfort than she did in bare feet.

What I was surprised to find left in the store was a good portion of the gun library. When money mattered, they sold guns with values in the 5 digit category. Like the quote from one of my favorite zombie films, "The only person that could miss with this rifle is the sucker with the bread to buy it."

I dug through the racks of expensive rifles and pulled out a Johann Fanzoi Sidelock in .500 Nitro Express. Why did I choose this rifle? Well, definitely not because I am familiar with the rifle, the caliber means nothing to me, and it sure as hell is not a practical PAW weapon. No, I chose this weapon because of the price tag. $50,000

I could have never afforded a gun like this in the BZ, so why not?

They only had 5 boxes of the ammunition for this rifle on the shelf and with a price of close to $400 a box, I wouldn't think they would have sold many of these.

One thing I am certain of though, if I come across any zombie elephants now, their asses belong to me.

Or any tanks. Yeah, I think I could definitely take out a tank with this thing. Maybe a hummer.

MID-OCTOBER 2010

Today, while driving along I-80, Derek saw something off in the distance. We stopped the truck for a more focused look. There, off in the distance was a farmhouse, which in itself is no big deal, we have seen thousands of farmhouses since we left Oregon.

The big deal is, how many farmhouses have we seen flying an American flag the size of the one flying over this place?

None.

Not to mention the fact that through our binoculars, this flag appeared to be intact and clean. That can only mean one thing: Survivors.

We found a road off the highway that got us on the right path for the farmhouse. Then we found the drive to the house and parked the truck. Derek said he would stay there, so I grabbed my rifle and asked Kimmi to come with me. We started to walk away from the truck when Derek honked the horn a couple of times. I turned around and he yelled out that he was signaling the farm.

Okay, it made a little sense to me.

Kimmi and I walked up to the house, me with my rifle in my hands and over my head and her walking right beside me. No, literally, right beside me. She was right up against my body.

Considering what the poor kid has been through, I can understand her latching on as tightly as she did.

We got to the fence when someone yelled out from the house to stop, followed quickly by, "What do you want?"

I introduced myself and Kimmi, mentioned Derek in the truck down below and told them we are nothing but weary travelers looking for some rest. We have our own provisions and are not looking for anything more than some fellowship.

Beth, as I learned shortly after, stepped out of the front door with an old double barreled shotgun aimed right at me and asked, "Is that your young 'un?"

I told her no, but followed up both quickly and briefly what the story was.

She said, "My name is Beth, upstairs is my husband Bob and the young man who is making your friend bring the truck up the drive is my nephew Eddie. Y'all might want to come inside."

Their last name was McCoy, I kid you not. Bob McCoy told us that they stayed out of the cities when things started going south and have been holed up here on the farm ever since. They have seen a few zombies out here but nothing too threatening. They don't even refer to them as zombies. They just keep calling them "those sickos." The closest house to them is 3 miles in any direction so I can see how they have not had much of a problem out here.

Kimmi latched onto Beth real quick. She must have sensed that there was nothing bad about these people because it was the first time in weeks she had let herself get more than four feet from me.

Bob took Derek and I for a walk around the farm, showing us the layout of the farm. Even in a post-apocalyptic world men like to show off their toys.

Their windmill provides enough energy for the basics in the house and at the same time provides enough pumping action to keep them in running water from the well. They have cattle, some sheep, plenty of chickens and a beautiful garden. All told, I would almost consider this place to be an ideal location to stay.

We had made the full loop around the farm when Bob told us we seemed like "nice enough fellers" and asked us if we would like to stick around for a while and help out. He was getting on in years and could not do as much as he used to be able to. Derek and I talked to each other briefly and decided we could stick around for a few days and go from there.

Bob wanted to see our truck; apparently Eddie had told him we had a massive gun in the back of it. We took him to the truck and dropped the fifty down from the ceiling so he could take a look at it. Like most people when they touch one of these things for the first time in their lives, he asked if he could shoot it. I grabbed some hearing protection for him and told him to shoot high over the top of the trailer.

Fortunately, only one of the ten rounds he fired did any damage. It took out the right side mirror on Derek's BMW. Well, it could have been worse. It could have been the gas tank.

We got back inside the farmhouse just in time to find Kimmi coming down the stairs. Beth had let her take a shower and had given her a sundress to wear. I just looked at her and told her, "You look beautiful little one!"

She blushed a little and it was the first time I had seen her start to warm up a little bit inside. Maybe in time we will actually be able to get her living on the inside again.

Tonight we ate a magnificent lamb stew and freshly baked bread, and later went to sleep in real beds. Both of them were things I never thought I would see again.

OCTOBER 2010

We have been here on the McCoy farm for the past twelve days. Since the McCoys have continued living just as they always had, they had been keeping track of the dates, and based on their calendar, we celebrated my 41st birthday a few days ago. Heather would have been 36 yesterday if she hadn't been, well, you know.

It's a little bit funny. When we first got here Derek and I agreed that we would only stay a couple of days and then get back on the road. Two days turned into four and four turned into twelve before we knew it.

Kimmi has been spending a bit of her time with Beth, learning to sew and cook. She even made us bread for the sandwiches we eat at lunchtime. The rest of her time is spent with me, talking about my family, my friends, and the daughter I lost years before the zombies rose up. I told her about the way my daughter had talked about me, and always wanted me to change to be the person she felt I needed to be in order to be her father.

Kimmi looks at Derek and I like we are something very special. When you consider how we found her, I can kind of understand that. She has even slipped a couple of times and called me Dad. That's okay, I kind of like that.

Derek and I spent the first few days going over our own stuff and Bob just let us do what we were doing. After a few days he started coming over, asking us if we would give him a hand with this chore or that chore. Of course, we are happy to help since we have been staying here, eating their food and sleeping in their home.

A couple days past I noticed something I thought was funny, Bob got up early in the morning like he tends to, and without saying a word to each other, Derek and I got out of our beds and helped him with the chores. I guess we are starting to settle into a bit of a routine here on the farm. That is not really a bad thing, is it?

It was that very same day, while helping to take the cows back out to pasture after milking; I looked down by the pond and saw Kimmi and Eddie walking around the pond, talking to each other. These two teenagers were reaching out to each other in the middle of the PAW, proving that life will go on, somehow, someway. I love seeing this because in the BZ high school hierarchy of things, this would have never happened. She was the "rich" prep girl and he the dirt poor farm boy. And yet here they are, finding each other.

The McCoys have been right about one thing, there are not many zombies out here. In fact, we haven't seen a single one since we arrived. I have asked about other survivors and have been told that there were some but they don't come around anymore and Bob and Eddie have been hesitant to go find out what happened as neither one of them are really fighters.

This morning, I took Bob and Eddie out back with a couple of M-4's and taught them how to shoot. We even covered some malfunction and transition drills. After lunch, I taught them how to break them down and clean them, stressing how important that is with these weapons.

Tonight after dinner I gave those rifles to them as a token of our appreciation. I told Bob it would be a sight better than that old Ruger 10/22 he had aimed at me when we first showed up.

Beth just sat there looking at us with a smile on her face for a moment before she hopped up and went into the kitchen. She came back out with a tray full of fresh baked apple pie. When she put the tray on the table she apologized to us. I asked her what the apology was for.

She said, "I don't have any cheese for this pie. My momma always told me that a piece of apple pie without cheese is like a kiss without a squeeze."

I picked up my pie, gave her a kiss on the forehead and walked out to the patio before anyone could see the tears welling up in the corners of my eyes.

As I walked out the door I heard her ask Derek if he knew where I was headed. Just as I started to step out of earshot I heard him say, "Most likely out to talk to his wife."

OCTOBER 29, 2010

Bob came to us early yesterday morning and said he needed our help, but this time would be different as he needed it off the farm. One of the components of the windmill generator was failing, and he needed a replacement part. He knew the shop that should have it in stock in Kearney, about forty miles east of our current location.

According to Bob's atlas, Kearney had a BZ population of almost 30,000 and another 6,000-7,000 University of Nebraska students. Add those numbers together and you have a recipe for a bad time.

Going into a possible horde of 30,000 zombies to find a part for a windmill isn't exactly on my list of priorities. However, due to Bob and his family having been more than generous to us since we got here we can't exactly say no.

I asked Bob for the part and if he could tell me where to find it and we would go and get it. Bob would not let us make the trip without him, he said he is the one that knows the shop, knows the part and knows the town. Without him, it would be as bad as trying to find a needle in a haystack, one surrounded by the undead. The faster we can get it and out, the better it will be for all parties involved.

Damn it! As hard as I try, I can't argue with that logic.

We left early this morning, Derek and Bob were in the truck and I was on my bike. When we got to the edge of town, we pulled over and I asked Bob to tell me where to go so I could scout things out before we go barreling into town. I also told them that if I don't come back in a half hour, to get the hell out of here and get back to the farm. Also, be ready to go if I come back fast—don't waste a second of time, just follow me.

What I found was a shitload of zombies. I had one of the MP-5s with me and took down as many as I could on the way in and on the way out but there were still going to be more than I wanted to fight through for a generator part.

I finally got back to the truck, left the bike on the roadside and climbed into the driver's seat of the truck. The road was relatively clear of wreckage so I knew we would be able to drive the truck right through the masses to clear a path.

I drove since I had just taken the scouting run and had a good idea of where to drive in order to avoid anything that might damage the truck. We were able to take out a good bit of the zombies in front of the shop before turning around and taking another run down the road. Then I turned the truck around and drove back up the road to the shop and backed it up to the doors, leaving just enough room for us to open the back doors. Derek opened the back while I lowered the .50 from the ceiling. Using their prybars, Bob and Derek knocked out the glass on the doors and then shined their flashlights inside the shop. There was no immediately detectable movement inside so they tossed their prybars back in the vehicle and brought their weapons up to ready and moved into the building.

With all of the movement on the sides of the truck it was difficult to make out what was happening inside the shop. Before they left I told them I would stay with the truck but they needed to go now, go fast and damn it, grab spares of anything he might ever need in the future. This was a one time only shopping trip, they needed to make it count.

I could see the horde building up through the portals on both sides of the truck. Even though there were only a dozen or so on each side of the vehicle I could almost feel the pressure from inside. It had to have been all in my head, knowing there was nothing more than a thin wall between me and dozens of zombies.

Then something happened that I had been praying would not, gunshots rang out from inside the store.

I heard a couple of bursts from an MP-5 along with a couple of pistol shots. It may have been nothing, as I now know, but at that time, Jesus, it scared the shit out of me.

I couldn't leave the truck. If Mr. Murphy really was along for this trip, then I needed to stay with it and make sure we had a way out of here.

Only a couple of minutes later they came running out of the darkness with boxes full of stuff. They passed them in to me and I told Derek to drive, crank the wheel hard to the right then punch it. As they passed through the back of the truck they looked out the portals and were able to clearly see all of the zombies just outside the walls. I told them to grab their hearing protection as they went by, it was going to get loud in a few minutes.

I then looked at Bob and told him to watch my back and be ready with his gun in case I go down.

Derek dropped into the driver's seat and pushed the pedal to the floor. Because of the damn weight of the thing it took us way longer to get up to speed than I would have liked. I started firing controlled bursts at everything I saw. Some of the damn things were so close to the truck that I was actually getting sprayed by goo as I fired.

Before I knew what was happening, a zombie more or less jumped into the back and grabbed my legs, pulling me down to the floor. Bob was shooting zombies the instant I hit my back but he wasn't shooting the one that had my leg. He couldn't hear me and I couldn't hear anything either.

I looked to my left and there was that Fanzoi Sidelock I had grabbed in Sidney. Since an unloaded gun in the PAW isn't worth shit, I knew it was loaded. I grabbed the rifle and pointed it at the zombie's head and turned it into a disgusting ball of mist.

I have a $50,000 zombie killing machine.

We were finally up to speed and I was able to pull the doors closed while Derek drove us back to where we had left my bike. He offered to drive it back but I declined. I really needed the fresh air and openness the ride offered.

We got back to the farm just a little bit ago. I took a shower while Bob went right to work fixing the windmill. When I came back downstairs he already had it repaired. I sat down at the table and looked at the box the part came in.

This little box that we just went through one hell of a fight to get our hands on, this little part that took him all of 5 minutes to install—$2.99

It's nice to know what my life is worth.

NOVEMBER 15, 2010

It has been a couple of weeks since the Kearney incident and while it should not be bothering me as much as it is, I keep seeing that damned $2.99 price tag every time I turn around.

Yes, I know the value of that part far exceeds that of its face value. I understand completely how nice it is having a better energy source than our few little solar panels are able to provide. I get it, I really do.

That does not remove the fact that I had to fight my way into and out of a small town filled with zombies for a little piece of machinery with a $2.99 price tag on it.

Has human life become so cheap in the PAW that a part for a windmill is worth more than human life? Or is it purely that the supply chain we got so used to in the BZ now involves human life more than it ever did?

I don't blame Bob, I really can't. The man is simply doing what he feels is right to take care of him and his family.

Hell, I don't even know who I can blame for this. Do I go back to the beginning and blame the government? Or do I just accept this as a part of the new world?

Honestly, I think that is ultimately the best choice.

Things happen now that would have made no sense a few years ago.

It is now up to us to do the best we can with what we have to work with and if it doesn't make sense, then we need to find the will to force it to make sense.

Everything happens for a reason, right?

DECEMBER 22, 2010

Derek and I have been talking over the past few weeks about getting back on the road. Our time here at the McCoy farm has been nice, but we both are starting to feel that closed in feeling.

Closed in? On a three hundred acre farm with the closest house being three miles away? Yeah, I guess I can see how that could happen.

We have talked to Kimmi about it and while she wants to stay with us, her relationship with Eddie has grown stronger than she realized. Sure, she and I still take our daily walks and talk about the past, present and future but she needs to have someone that can be there for her in ways we cannot.

Ultimately, it would be better for her to stay here and have the stability this home can provide. I will definitely miss her as she has become very special to me, almost a surrogate daughter. But Eddie is a good kid; he is very smart and has a good head on his shoulders. I am sure he will watch out for her once we leave.

Derek and I work in our spare time to get the truck set back up for the road, making sure our tanks are filled and everything situated inside.

Yesterday I pulled the .50 out and cleaned it, readying it for the trip, and made sure the ammo can is filled with a full belt.

Now all that we really need to do is talk to Bob and Beth and let them know we are leaving. We don't want to leave until the day after

Christmas as they are planning a special dinner that night, so we will wait until after dinner that night to let them know we will be leaving.

While I don't think they are the type of people to sabotage us so we can't go anywhere, I really can't take that chance.

DECEMBER 26, 2010

We told Bob and Beth this morning that we were going to be leaving. As I expected, they asked us to stay with them, but after explaining where we were coming from they were able to understand our reasons for leaving.

We both gave Kimmi hugs and kisses on the forehead and told her we will be back through in the future to check on her. All she said was that we "better come back."

We drove out of there about an hour after first telling them we were leaving. Neither one of us felt the need for a long, drawn out goodbye.

We drove east to just past Kearney where we took a road headed south. We figure that the further east we go we will be coming into higher populated areas off the main interstates. If we can avoid the major population centers, the happier I will be.

We stopped tonight in a little farm town called Athol, Kansas. There are CDC quarantine signs all over the place and no signs of excessive carnage or zombies here.

It looks like they had evacuated everyone out of town back when the outbreak first started. There is not much left here in town to scavenge. We did find some canned goods and a little bit of ammunition for my revolver and the shotguns but that was about it.

We hit a couple of houses just in hopes of finding more supplies but came up empty.

DECEMBER 27, 2010

Hiawatha, Kansas.

According to the sign at the city limits, population in the BZ was 3,000 plus.

Population today? 2,000 plus. All living.

We drove up to the town this afternoon and immediately came to a barricade stretching completely across the roadway. Unlike the roadblocks in Ogden, these were manned. The people looked a little rough around the edges but they seemed to be in good health and decent spirits.

We climbed out of the truck and they let us get about 30 feet from the checkpoint before they made us stop. We confirmed that yes we are armed but we are not raiders, and we are not looking for anything more than a safe place to park for the night, and that we would be moving on in the morning. As I looked around I was counting weapons and noticing nothing but sporting arms, hunting rifles and field shotguns. Not very well armed but it is better than trying to hold a town with nothing but spears.

They made us wait at the gate for thirty minutes or so before the Mayor could come out to talk to us. You have to love small town politics. Mayor Clark, as he introduced himself, talked to us for several minutes while we negotiated passage through their town.

We took him back to the truck and let him take a look at what we have. While I don't like anyone knowing everything we have I wanted him to see that we were situated with plenty of provisions for the two of us and we were not looking for anything from his town.

He finally told us we could enter for the one night and that he would like us to join him and his wife for dinner. We ate a meal of venison and canned vegetables with the Clarks. While we ate dessert we told them our story and the things we have seen so far in our travels across the country. They were revolted by the tales of cannibalism but I assured them that we have not seen any confirmed signs of that since we left Oregon.

In turn they briefly told us how they had escaped going to hell in a hand basket along with the rest of the country. Simple fact is, one of the town residents had a relative that worked for the Center of Disease Control down in Atlanta and spread the word about the vaccine as soon as she had confirmed it.

Hiawatha never allowed the vaccine into the town and the CDC contact kept the town off the government's radar somehow.

Since that time they have developed a town militia and have turned into one giant co-op. Everyone here contributes, and everyone is taken care of. They have a doctor that has taken on a couple of the nurses in town and is teaching them everything he can in order to have at least someone that can resemble a backup doctor. The farmers are all contributing to the well being of the town and in turn they get pretty much anything they need.

They have built more windmills around town than they ever had and have linked them all into the power grid and are subsidizing that electricity with solar panels. Apparently, the town was looking into going green long before everything went to shit so they already had much of the infrastructure in place.

More cities and towns across the country should have done the same thing when they had the opportunity to do so.

During our conversation the Mayor excused himself from the table to answer the door. He came back into the dining room a moment later and asked us if we would be willing to answer some questions for an impromptu town hall session. Seems people want to know what's going on outside of the town but nobody is willing to leave the safety of it.

We walked over to the town hall and spent the next two hours answering questions and telling our tale. I think they would have kept us going long into the night if the Mayor had not suggested that Derek and I needed some rest so we can leave tomorrow.

I can understand his desire for us to get out of town. They have made it this far because they have been so careful about letting the right ones in.

If it were my town, I would do the same thing.

DECEMBER 28, 2010

We bid Hiawatha, Kansas farewell this morning. Several of the townspeople came out to see us off, and even offered us some provisions for the road. The Doctor met us at the truck and gave me a wish list of things he would like to have. Mayor Clark told us that if we ever come back through this area, we have his blessing.

I think the thing that caught us the most off guard and made us laugh at the same time was when they brought us a package of letters and asked them to take them with us.

Derek and I immediately started laughing. We had to explain to them that we were both big time movie buffs' back in the BZ and this scene reminded us of one of the bad ones. When I told them I was definitely no Costner they even started to laugh with us. At the same time, I told them that while the world has gone to shit, if the opportunity ever arises to deliver even one of their letters, I will do it.

The Mayor gave us some final directions that would take us on a long loop south of St. Joseph, Missouri. He suggested we try to stay away from there as they had sent a scouting party there about 6 months ago. Six people went and only one returned.

We got in the truck, left town, and followed his directions until we got to Macon, Missouri, where we have parked for the night. This is another dead town, with not even the dead to disturb us. Seriously, this place is a ghost town.

We unloaded our bikes from the trailer and went for a ride around town. Eventually we made our way over to the hospital to look for medical supplies and that is where we found the prior residents – hundreds, if not thousands of corpses. Not chewed up, shambling along, just trying to make their way in the undead world kind of corpse. No, we are talking people lined up along the sidewalks as if they were instructed to lie down like they did for ease of future cleanup.

Seriously, it looks like the town lined up about a year ago and drank the proverbial kool-aid. In fact, I almost stumbled over the remnants of the containers of potassium chloride they used to do it.

Mass suicide of an entire town. Men, women and children of all ages, all dead. Educated people, police officers, doctors, teachers, everyone. They all lined up just like at Jamestown and they drank the fucking poison.

I went into the hospital to look for supplies while Derek went off to find a sporting goods store for additional weapons or ammunition.

I found the hospital to be completely occupied by the dead. As in, it looks they went through the hospital, floor by floor and killed every single patient here and just left them in their beds. As I scavenged I was able to get a case of IV fluid, tubing, first aid supplies and quite an assortment of medications. I also found everything on the shopping list for the doctor back in Hiawatha.

We are only a couple hundred miles away from there so we will likely just take this stuff back to them tomorrow.

While the town is dead I still don't like the idea of just leaving the truck and trailer and all of our belongings out in the open. Hopefully there is some kind of shop close by that we can just lock it up.

Derek did meet me back at the truck with several boxes of ammo and a couple of handguns in a backpack he had grabbed. He also said there is more ammo at the shop if we want to hit it again when we leave town.

UNDATED

We took the medical supplies back to Hiawatha a couple of days ago.

True to the Mayor's word we were welcomed back to the town and the doctor was extremely grateful for the supplies. They even offered us rooms at the motel for the night since it would be too far for us to go back to Macon that very same day.

Everything was fine, dinner was good, the company was good and when I first climbed into bed after a fairly hot shower, I thought I was in heaven.

Shortly after I fell asleep I was awaken by a group of men surrounding my bed. I didn't even get a chance to say anything before one of them hit me with something in the head. Before I passed out I heard one of them say, "The other one is not in his room!"

I woke up what I am assuming was the next morning. They had tied me to a chair on a platform in the middle of town square. I was surrounded by most of the town population and the Mayor was pacing back and forth in front of me.

Derek was nowhere to be seen.

I asked the Mayor what was going on, why were they doing this to me. He told me some bullshit story about how we had stolen from them on our last trip through and had come back for another round of theft. Since we had truthfully not stolen a thing from anyone in town I pleaded with the Mayor to use logic and reason.

He leaned in close to me and said that while he personally knows I did not steal anything, they have had a rash of thefts in the town and he needed to make an example of someone. Since he felt he needed every one of his citizens to continue to do the jobs they have been doing, he felt using me as his example was the right choice. Fucker even apologized to me for what they were about to do.

The sheriff stepped up with a hatchet and pulled the sleeve up on my right arm.

A single shot rang out and the sheriff dropped the hatchet because of the round through his shoulder. I looked up and there was Derek with his MP-5 scanning the crowd. Suddenly a voice called out from my left, "Cut him loose Eddie!"

It was Bob, covering the crowd with the M-4 I had given him.

Eddie came running up to me, his M-4 in one hand and a knife in the other. He used the knife to cut me loose then he helped me to stand up. I had him help me over to the Mayor because I had something to say to him. What did I tell him?

I grabbed him by the back of his neck and leaned in close before telling him, "Forget we ever existed, let us leave peacefully, or I will burn this entire fucking town to the ground!"

He had little choice but to walk us out to the checkpoint where I found that the guys had done their jobs. Every single person at the checkpoint was secured in one fashion or another. No casualties among any of them other than some bruised egos. Bob climbed into his truck while Derek retrieved my bike. I climbed into the back of the truck with the Mayor and told him to sit down and shut the fuck up. About 5 miles outside of town, I kept my word and let him out of the truck.

I climbed into the sleeping bag Bob had in the back and fell asleep while they drove us back to the farm. We have stayed here for the past couple of days so I can rest and recuperate.

Derek was telling me this evening that he was outside walking around when everything went crazy at the motel. He hid in the bushes and as soon as the crowd moved away from the motel he ran back in, grabbed his bike and got the hell out of there. He figured his best bet would be to get back here and get Bob. He drove all night to get here like some kind of two wheeled modern day cavalry.

I need to remember to thank him someday.

JANUARY 3, 2011

We took a couple of days after leaving the McCoy farm again to reach the truck. If it had just been me I would have likely pushed to get back to it. I was scared to death we would get back here and it would be gone.

On the way back, we clearly wanted to give Hiawatha a wide berth so according to Bob's directions, we headed south at Seneca, Kansas, then he wanted us to stop when we hit Coming, Kansas. That was when he said we could open the small package he had given us.

When we hit Coming we stopped the bikes and Derek opened the package. Inside was a GPS unit Bob had grabbed from the shop in Kearney. We plugged it into the cigarette lighter on my bike and while it took a while to find enough satellites to get us remotely in the correct area, it still worked. I am actually surprised that the satellites are still working up there. Your typical GPS unit back in the day would communicate with an average of six or more satellites which really helped to pinpoint your location.

Since this took us several minutes to finally lock in and get a solid signal, I would suspect that we are just hitting the minimum number of signals. That makes me wonder, have they stopped working or have they been dropping out of orbit with nobody there to give them the occasional nudge to keep in orbit?

Who cares as long as they still work well enough to get me where I need to go? We punched in Macon, Missouri and followed the GPS as we went. When we got to Atchison, Kansas, we decided to stay there for the night.

Derek kept saying there was something about Atchison that bugged him, but he couldn't remember what it was.

It wasn't until several hours of both of us hearing and seeing stuff, getting cold chills and all sorts of other crazy shit that Derek sat upright and said, "Oh shit! Atchison, Kansas, the most haunted place in the entire state!"

You know, being around in a world of the living dead, you would think that being surrounded by spirits of the really-dead would be no big deal.

Well, a BMW motorcycle goes really fast at two o'clock in the morning when two grown men are too freaked out to stick around anymore. We got back to Macon early this morning and were extremely happy to have found the truck where we left it and that it had been unmolested in any way.

We decided to catch a little sleep today instead of moving out right away. After the crazy shit last night in Atchison and our bat-out-of-hell ride out of that town, we are both totally exhausted. We slept most of the day, woke up to have a little dinner and then we just sat around tonight talking about what we wanted to do next.

I told him about this cave house that I had seen on the internet years ago down in Festus, Missouri. These people had spent a fortune turning this huge cave into a really beautiful house, but then could not afford the balloon payment on the mortgage. They were ultimately forced to sell their dream home. I figured since we are heading that direction, maybe we can go check it out.

Derek kind of quietly chuckled and said, "Well, I don't have any plans so why not?" Then rolled over and went to sleep.

Thanks Derek.

JANUARY 2011

The shop we have been parked in had three 55 gallon drums of gasoline sitting in the back corner under a dusty old tarp. Two were completely full and the third one that had a hand pump in it was almost half gone. By the time we got all the tanks filled on the truck and topped off all of our cans we still had one full drum left. I am pretty sure we both got hernias moving this thing into the back of the trailer but it is nice having another reserve of fuel.

We left Macon immediately and followed the trip I had laid out to Festus. It was only about a two-hundred-fifty mile trip but it took us close to 8 hours to get here. The highways were really covered with vehicle wreckage and other debris so we had to slow down to a crawl and take it easy, mostly because of the trailer. If we didn't have the trailer we could have made much better time.

Oh well, we need the trailer for the bikes and its hauling capability.

We were sitting there just south of Festus in one of the biggest cloverleaf intersections I had ever seen, waiting and trying to figure out our next move. Since this town had a population of almost 10,000 in the BZ, we wanted to scout it out before we go strolling into town.

We sat there on the overpass for 3 hours just watching with our binoculars, looking in all directions. There was a fairly big medical center directly ahead of us and we both saw the same thing, zombies. It was a good sized horde from where we sat and I really had no desire to hit it for supplies. Looking in towards down town, I kept seeing the same thing, zombies.

I think everyone in Festus turned into zombies. Honestly, I was seeing more here than I have seen since Kearney.

Derek finally turned towards me and asked, "So where's this house dude?"

That was when it hit me. I have absolutely no idea where the house is. It could be ten or twenty miles outside of town for all I know.

What the hell was I thinking? Oh, hey, there is a cave house in Festus, Missouri, let's go see it! Yeah, let's go find a private residence without a means of tracking down its location.

Jackass.

We went ahead and drove south for the night. According to our map the closest bridge across the river is south at a town called Claryville. Fact is, this is a one horse town now and I don't think much has changed since the BZ. There are only a couple of houses here and they were all empty so we chose the nicest of the bunch and will be sleeping here for the night.

Tomorrow we head off to God only knows where next. Maybe we will figure that out when we wake up.

JANUARY 2011

We have stayed the past couple of days here in Claryville just relaxing and doing some minor scavenging. We have not really found much in the few homes in the area, but at least it has been quiet here.

I do find it interesting that just up the road in Festus we saw thousands of zombies and yet down here we haven't seen a thing. We were not even finding corpses in any of the houses we had searched.

The only thing that I can think of is some of these areas must have been evacuated into the heavier populated areas and "safe zones" created by the government. Not only were they the cause of the outbreak but they helped to propagate it and nail the lid on the coffin of civilized society.

Civilized society. Does that even exist anymore?

We have only been on the road for a few months but we have seen rape, cannibals and zombies. Add in the good people, and the trying but misguided people, and it gives you a good insight into the psyche of mankind.

No, we have not seen much of civilized society on the road.

It's not really that hard to figure out either, as it really goes back to what I mentioned back in the beginning of this journal, the human factor. Not every man or woman is equal. You have those who are physically stronger and then you have those who are mentally stronger.

Look at the town of Macon. What appeared to be the entire town, committed suicide. Yes, we are speculating that fact, but we are also both intelligent men. Like the old saying, "If it looks like a duck and quacks like a duck, then it must be a duck".

Hiawatha... they are simply doing what is best for their community. While I may hate the Mayor for wanting to turn me into an example for his townspeople, I can understand why he chose to do what he did. Why harm one of your own in order to scare the town into compliance when you can do it to a stranger?

I took a road trip somewhat like this, minus the zombies, many years ago. In that trip I was able to experience both the good and the bad of mankind. But with an intact society, the bad were reigned in and controlled. Remove the binds of society and people will go apeshit as we have seen far too many times.

I was talking to Heather about this just very same subject the other day. She sat there and listened for a while until she told me her thoughts and fears. She said she is afraid for me, that I may be slipping too far, and may not be able to come back from where I am headed. She went on to tell me that she worries that my behavior will lead to me making a mistake, and while she would love to have me with her, I still have too much to do. When I asked her what I needed to do, she told me think about Kimmi.

I have not told Derek about this conversation yet. He already looks at me funny when I am talking to her. Yeah, like he never talks to Brenda when he thinks I am not looking.

Anyway, Derek and I talked a little after dinner tonight in regards to our plans and we are just going to hang here for a couple more days, enjoying the rest and relaxation.

JANUARY 2011

We finally left Claryville this morning and headed east. Derek and I had talked in the past about checking out Fort Knox, just to see if anyone was still around that area. We figure that if there is any significant amount of government left anywhere, that Fort Knox should still be heavily guarded. So, that is where we are headed to next.

Clearly this will be nothing more than a scouting situation. I have no intentions of trying to break into the vault or anything of the sort. I just want to take a look around. Besides, we still have a slight mistrust of the government and really don't cherish the thought of getting accosted by them if we get too close.

There were significantly more zombies on the road as we traveled through Illinois, Indiana and into Kentucky. Even staying away from the bigger cities we saw more than we had recently seen. Like I always told my friends that lived on the eastern seaboard, "You are fucked when the zombies come man!" Living in a larger population center may have its perks, but when the shit hit the fan, they were wiped out relatively fast.

As we continued driving I noticed something funny about Derek; without ever going out of his way to do so, he was clipping as many of the zombies as he could. All the while the look on his face never changed. He never grimaced, smiled, or showed any signs of emotion. I guess you could say it was therapeutic for him.

We got close to Fort Knox late this afternoon and decided to stop in a town called Muldraugh. The town had a few wanderers in the streets, but nothing we needed to be truly concerned about. After a slow drive through town we were also satisfied there were no survivors in the area.

We could see the base airstrip from where we were parked so we climbed up on the back of the truck to observe what we could for a while. We saw minimal activity on the base and figured it had to be zombies. They were too far away for us to be able to tell for sure though.

I told Derek to stay on the truck and cover me. I wanted a closer look. He said he would fire off a burst if he saw anything that would make me need to get out of there.

I made my way as quickly as I could to the fence of the airstrip, cut a hole and made my way onto the field. I lay down at the end of runway 15 and started glassing the base. Even from this distance I was having problems determining whether they were zombies or not. I low crawled up the runway, tearing my knees and elbows apart just so I could get closer. Finally, I saw one of them close enough to see him stagger and fall to his knees then get back up.

Zombies. Zombies in uniform. That tells me the base was likely overrun at some point in time. Convinced there would not be a military presence on the base I went back to the truck and pulled my bike off the trailer. Derek asked me what was happening on the base. When I told him nothing, he pulled his bike out of the trailer, he was coming with me.

We drove back to the fence, enlarged the hole and moved our bikes through the gap we had just cut. We made our way down the runway, bypassing the few zombies in the area as we left the airfield, and then finally connected with Bullion Boulevard and headed south for the gold depository.

After about a mile we could see the top of the building over the high fence.

As soon as we could see the gates we hit the brakes. At that point we could see they were closed and had been heavily reinforced, even more than they had been during the BZ. The tops of the fence had been restructured with a large overhang into the fenced area, apparently to keep anything on the inside from being able to climb out. Inside of the roughly 16,000 square feet enclosure were now what looked like thousands of zombies. There were so many of them that they were unable to do much more than bounce off of each other.

Jesus Christ.

They, the military, apparently filled the area with zombies to protect it until the government was able to stabilize and regain control.

I have to give them this, it was a smart idea.

Sitting there a little longer than we should have, our scent was picked up by the zombies and they started going crazy. Having been locked up in this area for a couple of years now without food they must be really hungry.

We fired up the bikes and got the hell away from the vault. We decided to stay the night here in Muldraugh, and will head out first thing tomorrow morning.

JANUARY 2011

We drove east today until we hit a town called Kermit, West Virginia which is just some little town in a valley. The population on the town marker had 209 crossed out and replaced with a big fat zero, just like most of the little towns we have passed through.

There were only a handful of zombies walking around the small town square, and we took them out quickly and easily enough. After that we set about scavenging what supplies we could. We kept finding burn marks and piles of charred skeletons scattered about the town. Either they took care of their own before evacuating, or it was the CDC and the military. Personally, I hope it was the town, but if they cleared the town of zombies why would they have left?

We found one house that was locked up tight as a drum. Bars on the windows and multiple deadbolts on both doors told me this was a house I wanted to get into. I used the last of my door breaching rounds to take the front door off the hinges.

When we finally got inside it was pretty clear what had happened. We had seen it all too many times. We assume the father, the largest male of the zombies resembled the father in the family picture on the wall, of the house had been bitten, locked up his family to secure them from the "crazies" outside and wound up consuming them one by one after he turned. I put him down for good with one stroke from my knife before locating and eliminating the rest of the family. Downstairs in the basement we found an AK-47, semi-auto but still a good weapon, and a couple thousand rounds of ammo all loaded into magazines. Along with a few cases of MRE's and a couple flats of bottled water we called it a good find and started to take everything upstairs. Just as I started up the stairs I noticed a box I had missed sitting high on the shelf. Opening it up I found several bottles of Maker's Mark bourbon, my brand.

We took all of the stuff we had found back to the truck and talked about tomorrow. I was heading for The Greenbrier Resort in White Sulphur Springs, West Virginia. This was the location of one of the U.S. Government Relocation Facilities, also known as The Bunker.

It was built back during the Cold War underneath a big fancy resort and was intended to provide enough space for the members of Congress and their families to go to in order to be safe from the nuclear missiles the Russians thankfully never launched at us. The secret bunker was eventually unveiled in the media thanks to some reporter that felt his name was more important than national security. After that it was abandoned and became a tourist trap.

Of course, we all know the government would have never abandoned it if they didn't already have another location ready to go somewhere. I would love to know where that one is.

I figure we can go check it out and see if anyone else had the bright idea. If nothing else, we will get to tour it for free.

JANUARY 2011

We drove the 150 some odd miles to White Sulphur Springs, West Virginia, in about four hours today, arriving here at The Greenbrier around noon. For the past few hours we have been clearing zombies out of the bunker.

The vault door was pushed closed but not locked when we got here. So we disconnected the trailer from the truck outside of the vault entrance and backed the truck up to the door. Since we had no idea of what would be on the other side when we opened it, I wanted to be ready with the .50.

Derek opened the door and as soon as it had enough momentum he jumped in the truck ready to drive away if need be. We had every light available pointed towards the tunnel and as soon as that door got out of my way, I saw them. It could have only been a dozen zombies in the tunnel but it looked like hundreds in the light and I opened fire.

Derek was watching over my shoulder with his MP-5 at the ready but we wound up not needing it quite yet. I emptied the entire can of ammo down the tunnel, dropping everything in my line of fire. Those zombies that did not take a head shot went down and would be easy pickings once we entered the bunker. Seriously, a rotted walking corpse is little match for the power of a .50cal round. Spines shatter, hips break, bodies get blown in two... it is a beautiful thing. Derek proceeded to back the truck up to the entry way blocking it off so nothing could come in or out unless they went through the truck.

We grabbed our gear including a bag of road flares and entered the tunnel, throwing flares ahead of us every few feet. Once we had moved up to the next flare, we lit another and threw it. We cleared each and every room killing dozens of zombies in each area. It got a little close in a couple of the rooms since we had already expended our flares and only had the cones of light from our flashlights with nothing but darkness at our peripherals. Derek even got jumped one time and grunted but immediately knocked the zombie to the ground, shot it in the head and said he was okay.

We finally got to the internal entrance to the bunker from inside the resort. The door was standing wide open. This certainly helped to explain all the zombies we were dealing with. Our guess is the staff and guests had run to the bunker in a panic and forgot to close a door. Talk about a monumental fuck up, it cost everyone in here their lives.

When we finally had the bunker clear, we ran back to the truck to replenish our ammo. We had blown through most of what he had taken with us and while we were certain we had it cleared, we were not quite ready to take the chance that we missed a few.

After a second run through the bunker, we were certain it was clear and we started searching for anything we might be able to use. I was in the dining room heading into the kitchen when all of a sudden the lights came on. Derek had gone into the power plant but I was certain there was no way he had gotten the generators running.

I ran to the power plant and found Derek standing there with a manual for a Hyperion Power Module in his hands. Damn! Someone had installed a mini-nuclear reactor here! These things have only started to become available in the past few years. This tells me that the government had never fully abandoned this place and was working on getting it back into a state of readiness.

If they had brought emergency power back to the bunker, what else did they bring? I ran back to the kitchen and opened the pantries. They were full of canned food and dried goods of every type. Looking at the manufacture dates on most of the foods I found them to have been made in the last two to three years.

I will bet you anything they were trying to get it ready for occupation because of the zombies but didn't get it done in time.

I checked the communications room and found all new equipment. The medical facility was fully stocked with more kinds of medicine and other supplies than I could have ever asked for.

The security center had a weapons locker filled with M-4's, MP-5's and M-9 pistols. What I had earlier mistaken for a display in the corner is really cases of ammunition for all three types of weapons.

This place was ready to complete its intended mission, to aid in the continuation of the government.

JANUARY 2011
ENTRY BY DEREK

Cole,

By the time you read this I will be long gone.

Remember the zombie that surprised me yesterday during the fight? Yeah, he got me on the right side of my chest. If we had checked each other last night like we should have, you would have seen it right away.

For not telling you that it happened, I sincerely apologize. You have more than earned the right to know. I think I finally understand why people in zombie movies always hid the fact that they were bitten from the other people around them.

The feeling of betrayal is immense. That I have let you down in some way is too great for me. After everything you and I have been through, I allowed myself to be bitten. Simply put, I am ashamed.

It is also fear that causes you to want to hide it. Knowing the instant you find out I have been bitten will prompt you to kill me, is terrifying. While I know there would be nothing personal about it, I know you would terminate me immediately. You have been a good friend all these years, and for one, I do not want you to have to put me down, and two, the thought of you staring me down over the top of your guns scares the shit out of me.

That is why I decided to leave. I know I should do the right thing and allow you to shoot me in the head. I am not quite ready to go yet.

I have taken my bike and I will go as fast and as far as I can before I get too sick to go any further. I know I will turn eventually and frankly, that is okay with me. As crazy as this may seem, I think I would like to try my hand at being a zombie for a little while.

Thank you for everything you did for Brenda and me. We would have never made it as long as we did without you. You have been and always will be a great friend and I wish you absolutely nothing but the best.

Keep up the good fight, it is what you do best.

Stay loose and stay safe,
Derek

JANUARY 2011

I have spent the last few days here in the bunker alone, cleaning up the mess and moving all of the corpses into one of the walk in freezers. I want to keep one of them clear just in case I ever get to a point where I am able to go outside and do some hunting. Last thing I want to do with a deer if I get one is to hang it in a corpse filled freezer.

It's eerily quiet here with nothing but a constant low level hum, the clicking of the compressors on the freezers and refrigerators and the whisper of the ventilation system.

This is not what I wanted.

I wanted to share this place with someone. I don't deserve to be here alone. Other people should be here with me. This bunker was built for 1,000 people and yet I am the only one.

I respect Derek's decision to leave but the selfish side of me wishes he had handled it differently. If he had let me know he was bitten but just wanted to leave I would have respected his wishes. And I would have been able to say goodbye.

Now I sit in this bunker with enough provisions to last me for years with no way for anyone to get in. I am for all intents and purposes in the near perfect situation with one inescapable caveat...

... I am alone.

UNDATED

Days have turned into weeks and for all I know weeks have turned into months. I have lost all track of time as I don't even know if it is day or night beyond these bunker walls.

I have kept myself constantly busy, doing something, lots of things, anything to stay busy. Little jobs like making sure that all of the bunks are made, the food inventoried, the guns cleaned and the ammo counted.

Heather and I have been having more and more conversations as of late. Most of the time she tells me I have been drinking entirely too much and need to slow down. I am alone in a bunker with nowhere to drive to and no job to get up for in the morning, what does it matter if I have a drink or three?

In regards to the alcohol, I would like to thank the government for making sure to bring in cases of booze for the Congressmen and their families and their children and their dogs. Why do they think they should get to drink expensive alcohol while they are burning our bodies in the streets?

But that's okay. Do you know why it is okay? Because I am here and they are not. I am drinking their bourbon and their cognac and they are rotting in the streets someplace.

They never made it here to the bunker, but I did!! Me, the old man with the bad heart! I have survived longer than they did. I even made it longer than the military with all their weapons, and satellites, and food, and tanks and big expensive airplanes.

ME!!!!

Derek came by a little bit ago and told me I should go to bed, that I need my rest. What the fuck is he doing here telling me to get some rest? He's dead like Heather, and Brenda, and Harley and the rest of the Kings. Fucking ghosts man. Nothing ever changes.

UNDATED

I woke up a little bit ago to some strange noises in the dining hall. Grabbing my weapon I made my way into the room to find someone sitting in a chair in the middle of the room. I started screaming at him to put his hands up and identify himself. He raised his hands in the air but did not speak to me. The closer I got to him I realized who it was, the missing left hand and the charred right hand... it was Harley.

I lowered my weapon and stepped up to him, asking him what the hell he was doing here. As he came into focus in front of me I saw the bullet hole in his head where I had shot him. I told him he was not real, he couldn't be real, I left him dead on the road in Oregon. He told me to sit down and we could talk for a while.

I did not know what else to do so I sat in a chair and asked him what he wanted to talk about. He told me he wanted to talk to me about my pain and when I asked him what pain he simply pointed at my chest. I tried telling him I am fine, I still have things to do, but he told me no, I had forgotten what I needed to do and maybe it was time for me to leave and motioned towards my pistol.

I asked him if he really thought it was the best thing to do and he said he would help me if he could. Together we raised my pistol to under my chin. He told me to close my eyes as it would help, so I closed them.

I locked the hammer back with my thumb then slid it into the trigger guard and onto the gentle curve of the trigger. Applying slight pressure on the trigger I felt the slack take up just before I got to the point that the trigger breaks.

I opened my eyes to thank him and Heather was sitting there in his place. I immediately took my thumb off the trigger when she asked me what I was doing. I tried to explain it to her but she got up and walked out of the room.

I threw the gun across the room into the darkness. I screamed myself hoarse and I have to admit, I have no idea how long I sat there crying.

UNDATED

I woke up today covered in my own vomit, an empty bottle of bourbon on the bed, and an empty bottle of valium on the floor.

How long have I been out?

I barely had the energy to get into the dispensary and start an IV on myself. After some oxygen, liquid vitamins, and health shakes I started to feel better.

I can't remember exactly what happened even though the signs are obvious that I attempted suicide. It's not that this is the first time I have considered it, but this attempt certainly came closest to being the most successful.

Looking at my last drunken journal entry makes me sick to my stomach.

I am not that man, I am stronger than that.

Like Derek said in his goodbye letter to me, I need to keep fighting.

Suicide is not the answer. It never was and it never will be.

I need to get out of this place, I can't stay here alone. If I stay here any longer I will surely try again, and will eventually succeed.

I am not ready to die, not quite yet.

UNDATED

I have decided to head west, back to the McCoy farm. It will likely take me several days to get there as I know things will be slower without Derek. Out here without someone watching my back at all times makes me nervous. It goes against everything we practiced and preached from the beginning, never go anywhere alone.

While I may be going back, I will not be abandoning the bunker. I intend to ask them to return here with me. It would be safer in all aspects for them to be in the bunker than on the farm.

I know they have not had any problems, but sooner or later the zombies will continue to spread out in search for food. Or, one of their neighbors that turned, may do that damn zombie instinct thing they do and come to their home some day. I don't even want to think about raiders.

I have spent the past two days refueling the truck and checking everything two and three times to make sure it is ready for the trip. All of my weapons are cleaned and ready to go, and the .50 has a fresh can of ammo. While I am hoping to make this a quick trip, there is no sense in going unprepared.

I figured out last week how to work the surveillance cameras here in the bunker so I at least have an idea when it is daylight out. Last thing I want to do is to go to leave the bunker in the middle of the night. This also gives me the opportunity to get my body regulated for life outside the bunker, adjusting for day and night.

Hopefully, I should be able to open the door, drive the truck out of the tunnel and close the door with no issues as the area immediately outside the vault door is clear. Once I open that external door though, all bets will be off and I may not be able to close it. Leaving the exterior door open might leave me with a hell of a fight on my hands getting to the vault door when I come back. Oh well, what is life without a challenge now and then?

UNDATED

I drove all the way Owensboro, Kentucky, today. I just have this funny feeling that I don't have much time for some reason. I feel fine, my heart is not giving me any issues or anything like that, I simply feel like there is a dark cloud hanging over me.

I think someone was following me, I can't be totally sure though. It started about 100 miles outside of the bunker when I caught a flash in the rear view mirror and figured it must have just been the sun glinting off one of the many wrecked and abandoned cars along the roadway.

Then, I started seeing what I am certain were vehicles swerving in and out of the cars. I even stopped a couple of times and glassed the road behind me but saw nothing moving.

Maybe I am just losing my mind more and more with the passing of each day. That is a very distinct possibility. I do know I have been parked here for a couple of hours and so far nobody has approached the truck.

Maybe I outlasted them? Maybe I made it outside of their area?

Maybe they realized I am not something to be disturbed.

Either way, I need my sleep.

UNDATED

I am sleeping in Macon, Missouri, again. At least it's a familiar place to me and I know the town is clear of any zombies.

I just can't shake the feeling that I am running out of time.

If I am in fact too late or whatever this feeling is, I would be absolutely no good to anyone if I am not rested when I get there.

At least the day passed without any of those hallucinations of people behind me.

Maybe I just needed the fresh air to get my mind clear. It is only my second day outside of the bunker, but I am already starting to feel kind of like a new man. Feeling almost as if I have been refreshed in a way. Maybe it is the fact that I am out here doing something more than just sitting in the bunker waiting for the imminent collapse of my sanity.

I keep thinking about the bunker and how things will be when I get Kimmi and the rest of the McCoy family back there. With other people inside with me, people for me to care for and protect, I honestly don't think it will be as destructive as it was for me alone.

UNDATED

I decided to make a more direct trip today, saving hours and miles worth of driving. Looking back, it may not have been the best idea.

Blowing through or attempting to blow through St. Joseph, Missouri, was a colossally bad idea. It used to be the largest city in northwest Missouri with close to 80,000 people. From what I saw, I think the population has doubled, which tells me that the government had used St. Joseph as an evacuation center. I tried heading north when I hit town but was soon forced to leave the highway because of too much wreckage. Every time I would turn down a road, I found myself heading into a horde of zombies too big to drive through.

I finally got to the outskirts of town and that was when I saw the camps. Thousands of FEMA trailers and just as many military style tents covered the open fields for as far as I could see. I will never understand the mindset of bringing all of these people into an area and telling them you will protect them. More people = more can go wrong. Our government never learned, let the people that want to take care of themselves do so. Never force a man from his home and disarm him in a time of emergency. Instead people should be allowed to be the defenders of their own homes.

St. Joseph was yet another reminder of the many failures from the past.

I finally found my way back onto the highway and headed south until I reconnected with Highway 36 and headed west until I hit Highway 7, taking me north so I could bypass Hiawatha.

A few hours later and here I am, back at the McCoy farm. Everyone is fine, if not extremely surprised to see me back, but even more so to find me alone. They tell me it has been more than six months since we left.

Wow. Six months? I guess I really did lose track of time.

Over dinner I told them about our trip, where we went, what we saw, and about the bunker. Obviously, I also told them about what happened to Derek.

Kimmi, who is now looking to be very much pregnant came over and sat on my lap, hugged me, and cried. She just sat there, rocking, and saying "You guys saved me, you guys saved me."

I looked at Bob and Beth and told them about the feelings I have been having. I also told them how I have always followed my gut throughout life and how it has never led me wrong. I asked them to please come with me back to the bunker, they will be safe and there are more provisions there for the five of us then we will ever go through.

Bob listened to my entire spiel and told me he would like some time to think about it. I told him that I feel that time is precious and should not be wasted, but I respect his wishes and will be giving him until tomorrow morning to make up his mind. With or without them, I am leaving in the morning.

UNDATED

Bob walked into my room yesterday morning and said three words to me, "Okay, let's go."

We spent all day yesterday gathering their essential supplies and loading them onto the truck. Beth started grabbing her linens but I told her to leave them. There was plenty of bedding back in the bunker, but Beth refused to leave her grandmother's quilt behind, so I told her she could bring it.

Bob brought out a cage full of chickens and a rooster and secured it to the roof of the truck. I have to admit, fresh eggs sure would be nice.

We loaded up the truck with all the fuel we could siphon out of their tractors and their truck. This was enough to give us another full complement of fuel.

Once in the truck we headed east to Macon, Missouri, again. I wanted to stay the first night there since the town has a shop that I remembered seeing a couple of times that would be perfect for Kimmi in her current condition.

We parked the truck at the shop and I walked Kimmi and Eddie over to the maternity shop and told them to go nuts. They were able to grab clothes for her and the baby along with a beautiful little bassinet that she said she just absolutely had to have.

Fair enough.

I also grabbed a box and filled it with children's books all the way up to about kindergarten level. They will come in handy.

As we left the store, I stopped and sent the kids toward the truck and grabbed one more thing that was hanging from the ceiling. It was a little red tricycle.

Heather told me that it was a good choice but I need to get going and that she would see me soon. I reached out to touch her hand, but as always, she just backed away and never quite let me get close enough.

I gave the trike to the kids when I got back to the truck and they were really excited about it. Kimmi wrapped her arms around my neck and hung there from me, crying. When she finally let go, she said that she and Eddie had talked about it and they would love it if I were to allow them to consider me to be the kid's grandfather.

I asked her if she meant godfather and she just shook her head and said, "No, Grandfather. With what you have done for me, that is how I feel about you. It's almost like you have become my father."

How does a person say no to that?

In my case, you don't. If she wants me to be the kid's Grandpa, then that is what I will be.

Christ, for someone in their 40's, I feel old.

UNDATED

We made it to Lawrenceburg, Kentucky, today. It is another one of those towns that had been evacuated and quarantined by the CDC. There was just a handful of zombies walking the streets, so I drove around town honking my horn to draw as many of them out of their hiding places that I could. As in the past, I would rather deal with them on my terms than theirs any day.

No more than a couple dozen came out to greet us so we simply took another slow drive around town knocking them down with the truck and driving over their heads. There is no sense in using ammo or physical energy when I have an armored truck.

Once we were confident no more were going to be coming out, we parked the truck for the evening. Beth was going to fix us dinner so Bob and Eddie went scouting for supplies.

This gave Kimmi and I an opportunity to talk while we stood guard. She told me all about how her relationship with Eddie had grown into real love and not just one of necessity. She even told me that she had not given herself to him completely until she was ready to. She said it made her finally feel in control of herself and was able to, for the most part, let go of what had happened to her back in Utah.

While we talked we had a few zombies come out of a building across the street from us so we took them out. She wasn't quite up to par with the head shots just yet, but she was coming along.

It was a great conversation. We talked about Heather, Derek, Brenda, and all the other friends I have lost and how I had missed out on saying goodbye to most of them. I told her how much it hurts to keep living while everyone around me has died. There are so many lost opportunities at goodbyes.

She promised me that she would let me say my goodbyes when the time came and she also made me promise to do the same for her.

You have my word little one.

UNDATED
ENTRY BY KIMMI

For weeks now, Cole's bag has laid there on the ground next to the closed vault door. It was only today that I finally picked it up and found this journal. I immediately sat down in the corner to read it. As I read through it I found myself learning even more about the man I knew, and I even got to learn more about the people he had lived with. Some of the parts of his story that have touched me the most was when he was unable to write for himself and his friends picked up his pen and carried on with his story for him.

To me, these are acts of loyalty for a very dear friend. Add in his tales over the past few years, and it shows how much he and his friends cared for each other. These people would have done anything in their power to help each other.

Because of my connection to Cole and having been able to read everything that happened to them, I now feel a connection to everyone he wrote about and feel that there would be a great injustice in the world if the rest of his story was not told.

The day after Lawrenceburg, Kentucky, was one of the longest days of my life since being saved on the highway outside of Ogden.

It was the day we lost Cole, the man who had become like a father to me.

We were getting closer to the bunker that day and I asked Cole more joking than anything, "Are we there yet?"

He just laughed that funny laugh of his and said, "It's less than a hundred miles to go and then we'll be there, little one. We will all be much safer after tonight."

It was about an hour and a half later when I noticed that Cole was looking in the rear view mirrors and was acting quite anxious about the things he saw. He kept looking from the mirrors to the odometer. It was as if he was wishing the vehicle could go faster.

I asked him what was wrong and he said the one word I wish I had never heard.

"Raiders!"

He told us he thought he had seen them behind him when he came through here the last time but had brushed it off due to what he was certain was a clouded mind.

This time, there was no doubt they were there. Cole said they were closing fast and there was a bunch of them. He just kept saying to himself, "We're so close, so close... "

I looked out the back window and could see six or seven vehicles about a half mile behind us, but they were closing that distance fast. Cole had Bob take over the steering wheel while he moved to the back of the truck. He handed out hearing protection before he lowered his big gun from the ceiling and told Eddie to open the back doors when he gave the word.

Cole looked at me and told me to get behind him. I sat down with my back against him and my hands pressed in as hard as I could to both sides of my head to protect my ears.

I could just barely hear Cole yell "Now Eddie!!!! Now!!!!" and the big gun roared.

I could feel the vibrations of the weapon coming through Cole's body and it felt like it was going to shake the entire truck apart. What may have been a couple of minutes later, something warm splashed onto my right hand and the side of my face. I brought my hand down and it was covered with blood. Beth started screaming, Cole had been shot, but he kept firing.

I turned around and got on my knees, I could see he had been shot in the left shoulder, very close to his neck. I started grabbing everything I could to put on the wound hoping to stop the bleeding. I looked beyond him at one point in time and could see that there were several burning vehicles on the highway behind us. I could also see that there was still one vehicle of raiders behind us. Eddie was backed into the corner firing a pistol towards the vehicle with his free hand. Cole was still shooting the big gun and yelling orders at Eddie and Bob. Then the gun stopped firing. He pulled the handle on the side several times before he reached under his bunk and grabbed that expensive rifle he had taken from the sporting goods store in Nebraska. He aimed it at the truck and before he could pull the trigger he was shot again. He fell down to the floor between the bunks but immediately fought his way up, put the rifle to his shoulder and pulled the trigger.

I am not sure where his shot went, everything was such an incredible blur by that time, but I do know that the truck all of a sudden turned to the right and started rolling, throwing the raiders out of the bed of the truck and all over the road.

Eddie closed the doors and I jumped on Cole, shoving pillows against his wounds, doing everything I could to stop the bleeding. He reached under the bunk and pulled out his medical bag and gave me proper bandages, showing me how to use them and secure them around him.

I asked him if he was going to be okay and his answer was, "Don't worry about me, little one, they haven't invented the bullet that can kill me!"

He directed Bob to the bunker and within half an hour we were there.

We pulled down to the entry to the tunnel and saw a small horde of zombies at the door. Bob said we could just turn around and use the big gun but Cole said it was broken. He asked Eddie if he was up for it and of course Eddie said yes. They grabbed their machine guns off the wall and Cole told Bob to drive the truck directly into the tunnel as soon as he got the door open.

He and Eddie then jumped out the back doors and started shooting. As I pulled the back doors shut I saw Cole shoot a couple of zombies that were heading straight for Eddie.

Cole made a run for the door, yelling at Eddie to cover him. He grabbed on to that big door and pulled it open enough for the truck to get into the tunnel. I looked at him out of the portal as we drove by and I thought I saw a flash of pain in his face.

Bob stopped the truck just inside the tunnel and Eddie ran inside, killing the last of the zombies out there as Cole started to push the bunker door closed.

I ran back to help him but he stopped me in my tracks. He gave me a strange look I had never seen and spoke the words I will never forget, "I can't come in, little one. Remember this, never let the wrong one in."

And then he showed me his arm. He had been bitten.

I cried, begged, screamed, and pleaded with him to come inside but he wouldn't do it. He just kept saying "You know I can't!"

Eddie grabbed me from behind and tried to get me to understand that what Cole was saying was true. Bob even asked Cole if he wanted him to shoot him and Cole said no, he still had things to do before he was ready for that.

Cole then took my hand and said, "I don't have much more time, little one. Heather is calling for me right now. I hear her, it's time for me to go. Remember what you said? You told me you would give me the chance to say goodbye."

I told him how he saved me in more ways than one that day, and now, he has saved me again, I told him how much he meant to me and that none of us will ever forget him. I leaned in and kissed him on the cheek, then hugged him as close as I could and I whispered goodbye.

Bob shook his hand and thanked him for everything he had done. Cole told Bob he had something for him as he dug around in his bag, He pulled out this flattened little cardboard box and handed it to Bob who took it in his hands and looked at it. Bob said, "This is from the generator part we got back in Kearney, isn't it?"

Cole nodded his head and said, "It was worth it Bob. In the end, it was worth it."

Eddie thanked him for bringing me into his life and promised to make his sacrifice worthwhile.

Beth gave him a big hug but didn't say much. I don't think she was capable of saying anything at that point in time.

Cole took off his guns and his knife and handed them to me along with his bag and told me they were mine now, to take good care of them.

I hugged him one last time. I never wanted to let go. He gently pushed me back, kissed me on the forehead and passed me to Eddie.

Then he pushed the door closed and Bob spun the handle, locking the bunker door.

JUNE 14, 2012
ENTRY BY KIMMI

Cole Derek McCoy came into this world six months ago. He is a healthy baby boy and I can only hope that he grows up to be the same type of man as his father and his two namesakes.

His delivery was okay, better than my previous child and while I am glad it happened, I hope to not have any more children. I kind of freaked out when Beth lifted him up so I could see him and did not settle down until he was in my arms. As soon as he was there though I knew nobody would ever be taking him from me. He took to nursing right away and has fed like a little piglet ever since.

Eddie came to me a couple weeks ago and asked me if I wanted to see something. He has been reading the manuals that are all over this place and has figured out the basics of how much of it works. He took me into the security room and had me sit in front of the monitor, and then he flicked a switch. The screen came on with a funny green hue but there was Cole, just kind of standing there gently rocking, left and right, left and right.

Eddie pointed out that Cole had apparently closed the exterior door before succumbing to his wounds and turning. We guess this was to prevent outsiders from knowing that there was a bunker down here. Even in death he was keeping us safe.

Fortunately because of the green, Eddie says this is because it is a night vision camera, Cole looks okay. His face is not all chewed up so that helps me look at him without thinking of the pain he was in.

Eddie flicked the switch for the audio and told me to talk to him. I said, "Hello?" and Cole started looking around, softly growling. I started talking to him and he just kind of growled a little bit every time I spoke. While it was creepy at first I have grown accustomed to hearing this voice instead of his true voice. That is not to say I wouldn't give everything I have to be able to talk to him again.

I have started coming in here now on a daily basis and talking to him a little bit. I tell him about Little Cole and every little thing he does. I tell him every day that we all miss him and how everyone is thankful for what he did. I also tell him that we tell his story to Little Cole and how he has a mommy and daddy that love him very much because of these two special men.

Most of the time, Cole just stands there rocking back and forth but I swear today he looked directly at me and Little Cole through the camera. Eddie says it was just a coincidence but I do not want to believe that. I was introducing Little Cole to him and calling him Grandpa when it happened.

No, I believe that there is something left of Cole out there and that in his own little way he is still standing guard and protecting us. If that is what I need to believe in to make some sense out of all this, then that is exactly what I will do.

Bob and Beth have taken to watching movies on the theater system that was installed here in the bunker. It looks like they had stocked every single movie ever made to keep the leaders entertained.

I have been reading books from the library. In fact, I started with the very first one on the shelf and have been reading them in that order. Fortunately, it is not all political science books and boring crap like that. Books with covers proclaiming spots on the New York Times Best Sellers List are on the shelves as well.

I swear today that I heard a phone ringing, but by the time I got into the communications room there was no ringing and no dial tone of any sort on the phone panel.

I guess being in a location like this can kind of slowly drive you a little insane, just like Cole had said.

While I may miss the sunlight and the fresh air, it is nice knowing that I will be able to raise my baby without worries of some crazy raiders or zombies eating him.

We are least able to keep track of the calendar again. Eddie had figured out a way to sync the time on one of the computers with a server someplace, so as far as we know, the date is now correct here in Cole's journal.

AUGUST 9, 2012
ENTRY BY KIMMI

Today was looking to be just another normal day in the bunker. I was in the security room for my morning talk with Cole and Little Cole.

Eddie was doing his system checks, making sure that things were running normally and Bob and Beth were taking care of their chickens and the little hydroponic garden that Eddie had helped them set up.

Yeah, just another normal day in the bunker, until the phone rang. I grabbed Little Cole and ran for the communications center and answered the phone.

The man on the other end of the line identified himself as Captain Richard Jeffers of the United States Air Force. He wanted to speak to the person in charge.

I told him he could talk to me and he asked "Well, who are you?"

I told him my name and that I am a survivor.

He asked if this was in fact the Greenbrier Government Relocation Facility.

I told him that it was in fact the Greenbrier bunker but there were no members of the government here.

He asked how many of us there were and I told him there were only the four of us and a child. He told me to hold and he would call right back.

By this time everyone was in the room with me, wanting to know what he said. I was in the process of telling them the gist of the conversation when the phone rang again. It was the same Captain so I told him I was going to put him on speakerphone so we could all hear what he had to say.

He told us the United States government was getting a handle on the situation in the southeastern corner of the country, in Florida. With assistance from Cuban armed forces, they had cleared most of the state and had been in contact with multiple groups of survivors all over the east coast. Bob asked him how they had been clearing the state and how they had done it with bigger cities like Miami. The Captain's response was chilling, "Low elevation fire bombing sir. It has proven to be very effective. Everything burns so we lose the cities but regain the ground."

Captain Jeffers proceeded to tell us that within the next six to eight weeks they should be within helicopter range of the bunker and could evacuate us to the safe zone which is now located on the island of Cuba.

Guantanamo Bay, Cuba, had been the seat of the American government for the past few years. Apparently, the Secretary of Defense had been on the base for an inspection when everything went south, so the President asked him to stay there for his safety.

Air Force one was making an emergency flight to Cuba with the President on board a couple of years ago but they never arrived.

There had been constant communication with other government continuation bunkers, but sometime over the last year, they lost contact with the Executive Branch bunker. Based on that fact, the Secretary of Defense was now the de facto President of the United States.

The fact that we had answered the phone was a total fluke as the Captain was simply going through the list of numbers over and over in hopes that someone would answer. He has admitted to me that he had not expected anyone to pick up at our location.

Bob asked him how he was able to call us to begin with and was told that all continuity bunkers were hardwired for communication. Supposedly, even in the event of a nuclear apocalypse they would have been able to communicate with each other.

Captain Jeffers gave us instructions on how to contact him in case we needed anything. He has also assured us that they will be doing everything in their power to get us any aid they can. He told us to sit tight and he will call us tomorrow and every day thereafter at the same time for situation reports.

We're going to be rescued!

SEPTEMBER 16, 2012
ENTRY BY KIMMI

True to his word, Captain Jeffers has called us every day at the same time with situation reports.

And every day, we have a list of questions for him that he has answered to the best of his ability. Over the past few weeks these are some of the answers he has given us:

Yes, it was a global event and not just restricted to the United States. Even today many countries are not responding to communication attempts. Whether it is because of infrastructure failure or because there is no one left, nobody really knows for sure.

From the few remaining satellites available and under control, imagery has shown that many countries' populations were completely obliterated.

As for Americans, they have a database of approximately 75,000 survivors outside of the government and military. 75,000 out of close to 300,000,000 people. Using this journal I was able to give the Captain information on some of the groups of survivors Cole had come across in his travels. He appreciated the information and once the military is able to move west they will take this information under advisement.

I have asked the Captain if they are aware of the raiders and the cannibals. He confirmed knowledge of them and that the President was well aware of it as well and had already passed down an Executive

Order. Anyone having been found to have survived by willfully consuming human flesh is to be considered an enemy of the state and is to be treated as such.

I asked Captain Jeffers what that meant. He just said, "Our orders are to shoot and kill every one of the infected we come across ma'am."

I told him "Good, this is no time for due process."

He said, "No ma'am, due process right now is a bullet."

As of the phone call this morning, the military was closing on Jacksonville, North Carolina, which, according to the Captain, is the home of Marine Corps Base Camp LeJeune. With the air field and the small amount of Marines that are still there, they should be able to reclaim it intact without firebombing it. It seems there was a small contingent of Marines that had been able to keep the base from being completely overrun.

What that means for us, is that in a few days we will be within helicopter range.

Just a few more days, Cole, just a few more days.

OCTOBER 14, 2012
ENTRY BY KIMMI

Cuba.

This is one of those places I never thought in a million years I would ever see. Now here I am, temporarily living amongst a small ragged group of survivors. Not that 50,000 people is a small group, but when you count that against the BZ population, that is a very small group indeed.

It was two weeks ago that the rescue chopper finally came for us. Captain Jeffers was on the phone with me when the chopper was inbound. He said it was his way of making sure that we knew we were opening the doors for the right people. They have had a few unfortunate mistakes in the past and they have quickly learned from them.

He did apologize to us because there would be some fairly rough treatment and initial interrogation but it should not take too long.

He said it was for security purposes, they simply needed to make sure we are who we say we are and that we are not infected. He also said that we should not be armed when they arrive, again, for security purposes. However, the President had decreed that based on the second amendment combined with the current population of the undead, that any personal firearms would be able to be retained.

However, any military firearms that had been scavenged during the siege would need to be confiscated.

While all of those conditions were fair to me, I did ask for one special condition. Over the past few weeks, I had been telling the Captain some of Cole's stories and especially what he did to get us safely to the bunker. I told him how Cole had protected us all and how he was still standing guard over us. I told Captain Jeffers about Cole and where he is located and I asked that he be restrained but please don't destroy him. Captain Jeffers has assured me that he has personally spoken with the President and based on Cole's activities, his corpse would not be molested. However, once we are in the air, the area will be firebombed and any previous arrangements would be null and void. I told the Captain that once that is the case, Cole would understand and his job would finally be done.

Eddie took over the phone and I went into the security room for one final talk with Cole. He stood there seemingly listening to me as I told him that the military was going to be opening the door soon and that he needed to be good and not bite anyone, they were here to help us.

Eddie yelled out, "They have landed!"

I told Cole to be good, that I had been given the word of an Air Force Officer that he would not be harmed, but he had to be on his best behavior.

The exterior door opened and in swarmed several heavily armed military men. Two of them had long sticks with chains looped over the end. Cole turned to face them and as soon as he did they slipped the loops over his head and they were able to securely hold him. Two others stepped up behind him and handcuffed his hands behind him. One of them kicked him behind the knee causing him to drop to his knees before I heard one of them say, "We should just shoot this fucker here and now!"

I hit the button on my microphone and said, "I heard that, gentlemen, you have your orders, he is not to be hurt!"

Eddie called out, "Captain Jeffers says Cole is secure, we can open the door!"

Bob was waiting at the door . He turned the handle unlocking the door and gave the door a push. Hands grabbed the door as soon as they could and quickly pulled it open.

Captain Jeffers wasn't kidding when he said there might be some rough handling at the beginning. We were all grabbed and dragged outside, stripped naked, handcuffed, shoved to the ground and every inch of our bodies were thoroughly examined for any signs of infection. While this was going on, someone I can only assume was a psychiatrist was asking us questions, maybe trying to determine our sanity levels? I don't really know.

This entire time, Cole was standing there watching us intently emitting a very low growl. Every time one of them would touch us roughly he kind of lurched towards us just to be jerked back to where they originally had him.

Once the questioning was done, they covered us with a powder that they said would delouse us. Then they burnt our clothes and gave us scrubs to wear. Next, they told us that if we had the ability to bathe, we could go back into the bunker and do so as they were done with the fumigation process.

I told them we been able to shower all along and were quite clean inside the bunker but they told us it was just a precaution.

I walked back into the bunker and Captain Jeffers was still on the speakerphone, so I told him everything was done, they were letting us clean up and gather our personal belongings.

He told me that he had spoken with the President directly about our situation and was instructed that Cole was to be brought to Cuba with us for proper burial arrangements.

I told the Captain I appreciated that but I doubted the military personnel would go for it. When he asked what I meant I told him about the way they were treating him. He told me to go grab the Lieutenant in charge and bring him back to the phone. I wrapped a blanket around myself and went out to the military men and asked the Lieutenant to come with me, he was wanted on the phone.

Inside the communications room he spoke and said "Lieutenant Ramirez here sir, how can I help you?"

Another voice responded, "This is the President speaking Lieutenant. That infected American is to be brought back to Cuba for a hero's burial, is that understood?!"

"Yes sir!"

"Good, then make it happen and stop being a jackass!"

"Yes sir!"

As the Lieutenant walked out he was mumbling something about "fucking zombies". I thought it was funny myself.

Captain Jeffers came back on the line and told me we needed to get a move on and he would see me when we get to Cuba.

Our personal belongings were brought out by the soldiers and all of the military weapons were taken out and placed in a pile. By the time I got done bathing and dressing both Little Cole and myself, all of our stuff was outside. They told us to grab what personal weapons we wanted to take but instructed us that the ammo would be locked in ammo cans and secured at the front of the helicopter. Again, this was purely for security reasons.

The soldiers were writing down the serial numbers from all of the weapons for inventory as one of them explained to me. Then he leaned in and whispered to me, "Typical military bullshit if you ask me!" Then he and a couple of the other soldiers placed explosive devices in the piles of military weapons while the others rushed us toward the chopper.

When the bombs went off, they didn't really explode, they just kind of burned really hot. One of the soldiers saw the look on my face and said, "Thermite! It will melt much of the weapons' components, rendering them inoperable!"

We climbed up the ramp of the chopper and took off. Within a couple of hours we were landing at this really big military base that must have been LeJeune and were rushed onto a big airplane one of the soldiers called a C-130.

We ate MRE's and talked to the soldiers on the plane during the flight, telling them our stories and I told them about Cole, why he was there with us. One of them joked and called him my Guard Zombie. I told them that Guardian Angel was more like it.

Several hours later we were told to prepare for landing; below us was Guantanamo Bay, Cuba.

Captain Jeffers met us at the plane and directed a team of handlers to take Cole to "the cages". He then gave us passes that would enable us to see him before he was terminated. Then, he personally directed us to the tents that were going to be our homes until something more permanent could be established.

We have been here ever since and while I have gone to see Cole every day, they have not designated a time for us to terminate or bury him. In this situation, it's nice to know that even now bureaucracy is slow.

DECEMBER 1, 2017
ENTRY BY KIMMI

Cole,

This is the last letter I will be writing you here in your journal.

It has been five years since we were rescued from the bunker and I wanted you to know everything that has happened since then and how we are rebuilding as a country.

Since Cuba had prevented the spread of the infection in their own country, they have been the ones to help the world rebuild. One of the Marines was telling me one day that even before all of this happened Cuba actually had one of the best medical systems in the third world.

With most of our physicians, engineers and teachers having been killed during the siege, Cuba has provided not only their people to assist us but have given us educational assistance so we can continue to grow on our own.

I became a teacher after graduating from an accelerated program. It was so hard learning to speak Spanish at the same time I was learning to teach, but now I have my own classroom and students here in the New USA.

Everything is New This, or New That these days. In a way it is kind of silly but they feel the best way to rebuild is to start from scratch.

For now, most of the remaining population has been moved to the Washington, D.C. area. However, there are pockets of survivors out there that have been allowed to stay where they are, as long as they are able to prove their self-sufficiency. Considering the fact they have survived as long as they have without government assistance, I think the question is moot in most situations.

President Bishop had decided he wanted to spare Washington from the firebombing at all costs as it was the site of our heritage and would be the perfect place to rebuild. So the armed forces coalition spent weeks clearing out all remaining zombies from the city and surrounding areas

You should see it though. It is almost like the old west these days. Since we have been unable to train a big enough workforce, and are refusing to pay the exorbitant fees for fuel being demanded by the countries that have it, we have resorted to bicycles and horses. Nobody travels very much these days.

There are still vehicles available for official transportation, but even they do not get used unless it is absolutely unavoidable.

People are now required to be armed at all times from age 10 and up. We have to be, as there are still plenty of zombies out there roaming around. We still see them walking down the streets at times. Even with the clearing operations here in Washington it was impossible to get them all, especially more so, when you consider that they seem to be drawn to this area now because of the concentration of human life.

It is an odd life at times. They are still working on walls around the city and have been for the past couple of years. We have random checkpoints in the streets, and every day before I start my class, each of the children is inspected from head to toe for any signs of bites.

When you stop and look at what has become of our society, ultimately, in a way, it is a good thing. You once said to me that an armed society is a polite society. That has been so true, Cole! There have been very few reported crimes since we were all relocated here from Cuba.

Everyone is finally working towards the same goal and that goal is the survival of humankind. I honestly believe that with us having purged society of the raiders, that we removed a vast population of people that would have been destructive of that goal. You once said that the people that became raiders were the people that were the dregs of society to begin with. A sane and normal person does not up and decide, hey, I'm hungry for human flesh. It takes a sociopath to begin with and that is why the predators from society are the way they are.

In sadder news, Bob died a couple of years ago. He went to sleep one night and simply never woke up. In the months before he died, he had overseen the planting of communal gardens in The Mall right there in the middle of D.C. Like I said, things are different now. The paradigm shift has been amazing. You really should see this garden though Cole, it's called The McCoy by most people, but officially it is the Robert McCoy Memorial Garden for the People. I guess you could say it has a Socialist ring to it.

Beth is doing fine and still lives with us in the condo that was given to us here at the Watergate hotel.

Eddie has received a degree in Engineering and is constantly working on new ideas to make things work with what we have available to us. He is really good at his job and he is making things better for everyone all the time.

Little Cole will be turning 6 years old in a couple of months but cannot wait until he turns 10. I have promised him that your pistol, the one that has been on my hip since the day you gave it to me, will be his first firearm. As it is, I have seen him playing out in the yard with sticks, and every time I ask him what he is doing, he tells me he is killing zombies just like his Daddy and Grandpa Cole did.

As for you, well, we brought you with us when we were relocated. The President made special arrangements for you as he had special plans for you.

The day that you were finally terminated was the day that you were laid to rest at Arlington National Cemetery. They said that with your prior military service combined with your actions during the siege, that if that didn't rate you a plot in Arlington, then nobody deserved one.

They called you a hero and gave you a full military burial, Cole. Then they had me give the epitaph since I knew you better than anyone there, but I couldn't. I did tell them something you said to me that last night in Lawrenceburg, Kentucky. You told me that you were no hero, you were just a man doing what a man should do. I'll never forget that the President stepped up to me and hugged me as I stood there crying, trying to tell the story. He told me something else that you had said to me years ago, almost word for word. He said, "A hero is an ordinary man, placed into an extraordinary situation and rising to the occasion with exemplary style. This man was a hero and an example for us all."

They saved The Greenbrier Resort instead of firebombing that area and have renamed it The Helman-Koch Resort in honor of you and Derek. This happened after the President read your journal. He said if you two hadn't "taken such a damned crazy route" across the country he would have renamed an interstate after you two. But since you did, he claimed the resort under Eminent Domain and named it in honor of you.

You would also be proud to know, Cole, that your journal has been placed in the New Smithsonian so future generations can see what you saw and learn from our past mistakes. They have it on display with replicas made available to anyone that wants one. I know that I will be making your journal required reading for all students in my classes.

The Smithsonian, even asked me if I would be willing to give up your knife for the display. I let them have it long enough to create a replica but I am not letting them have the real thing. This knife is on my hip almost sixteen hours a day and has become a part of who I am.

About three years ago, I was called to the White House for a meeting. There was a gentleman in the office that for one reason or another, he reminded me of you. His name is Ezra Blake and he had been asked to retrace your steps in order to bring back anything of yours that you may have left behind. The President told me that I need to understand that the way he has handled your situation has been political posturing. He went on to say that the fact is, you did nothing more than hundreds of other people did to survive. The difference is, you documented everything. He told us, "this new country is in need of new heroes in order to help the healing process" and he wanted Mr. Blake to help finish the job that you started.

While I did not like what the President said about you, it makes sense. We do need heroes and if the best we can do is to create one out of you, then so be it. In my heart though, you are a true hero.

I saw Mr. Blake him again about six months ago. He just showed up one day at my door and gave me one small picture of you. He told me that he had returned with significantly more than that, but the Smithsonian had taken everything else from him for their display. He also told me that another team had located your friends Gabe and Lenny in the exact location they had left you in your journal. According to him, they were all doing fine and wanted to stay where they were. Mr. Blake went on to say that the news of your passing was met with great sadness. He left shortly after and I have not seen him since.

Apparently the Smithsonian will have your display completed sometime in the next year. I have been asked to be there for the dedication and of course I will be there.

Until then, I will never forget your face, not the zombie face I saw last, but the face of the man and his friend who saved me on the roadside.

The face of the tired old man that last night in Lawrenceburg…

The face of the man that fought courageously to save us all during a mad dash to safety…

Or the face of the man that knew he was going to die, yet, who desperately needed to say his goodbyes before closing that door.

No, that is the face of the man who gave me back my life, who gave me hope, who helped me find my husband and the man who gave us all a future.

We will never forget you or any of your friends who helped you on your journey through those darkest of days.

You truly were the Kings of the Dead.

All my love,
Kimmi McCoy

Permuted Press

delivers the absolute best in **apocalyptic** fiction,
from **zombies** to **vampires** to **werewolves**
to **asteroids** to **nuclear bombs** to
the very **elements** themselves.

Why are so many readers turning to
Permuted Press?

Because we strive to make every book
we publish feel like an **event**, not
just pages thrown between a cover.

(And most importantly, we provide some
of the most fantastic, well written, horrifying
scenarios this side of an actual apocalypse.)

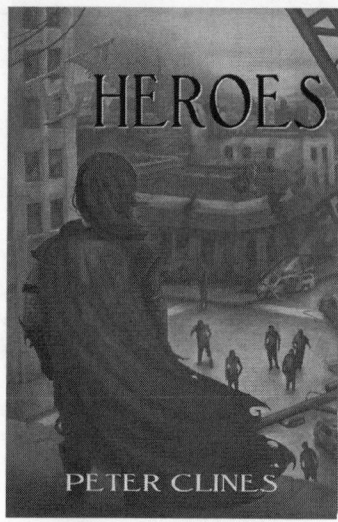
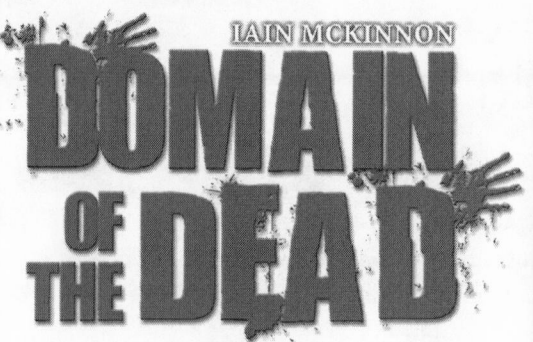
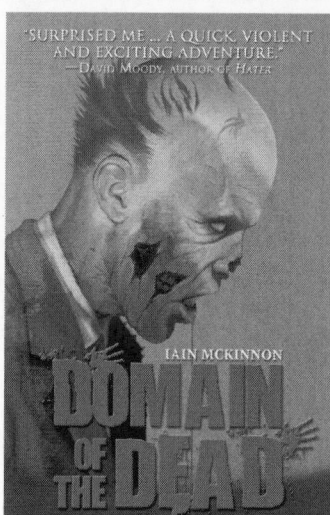

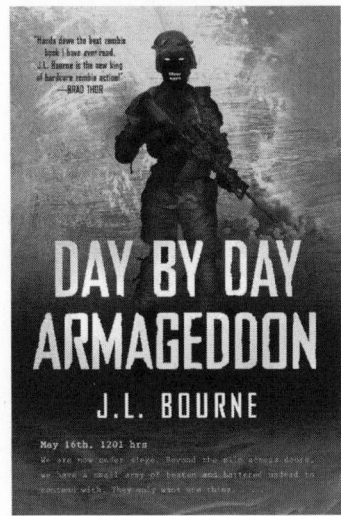